THE DEEP CODE

The landscapes of *The Deep Code* range from rural Mississippi to the deserts of New Mexico, the mountains of western Montana, and the tourist traps of the Florida Gulf Coast. These eight stories tell of desperation and perseverance in the face of generational struggles. In the title story, a recovering alcoholic tries to preserve what's left of his fractured relationship with his son, while trying to free himself from another of his step-father's get-rich-quick schemes. In "The Golden Horde of Mississippi" a young woman butts heads with her grandmother over the appropriate way to honor her dead, heavy-metal-loving cousin, while in "Escalation Dominance," a Los Alamos nuclear weapons scientist tries to embrace the child of her husband's affair with a local hippie girl. With unflinching love, these stories explore characters bestowed with little more than the refusal to succumb to their own bad choices in life.

The Deep Code

stories by
Charley Henley

China Grove Press

For my mother,
Patricia Henley

Copyright 2016 by Charley Henley
All rights reserved. No part of this book may be reproduced in any form without the permission of the publisher, except by a reviewer who may quote brief passages.

FIRST EDITION

China Grove Press / IsoLibris Publishing
ISBN 978-1-944106-07-2

This is a work of fiction and although places and world events have been depicted truthfully, all characters are the product of this author's imagination. Any relation to persons, living or dead is purely coincidental.

Acknowledgements

These stories, sometimes in slightly different form, originally appeared in the following journals: "The Golden Horde of Mississippi" first appeared in *Best New American Voices 2005*. "In a Valley of Dried Bones" first appeared in *The Greensboro Review*. "The Nazi Method" first appeared in *BULL {Men's Fiction}*. "Satellite Mother" first appeared in *Copper Nickel* and has been previously published by Amazon Publishing.

The author gratefully acknowledges the support of the College of Arts and Sciences and the Department of English at the University of Cincinnati. Also, he wishes to thank the following people whose advice has been critical in the development of these stories: Mark Winegardner, Elizabeth Stuckey-French, Will Belford, Stuart Flynn, his father Charles Henley, his mother Patricia Henley, and, his wife Trish Thomas Henley. Trish has read and edited each of these stories countless times, and without her input, the author doubts that any of them would have seen the light of day.

The stories:

1. The Deep Code 1

2. The Golden Horde of Mississippi 25

3. Satellite Mother 48

4. In A Valley of Dried Bones 67

5. Escalation Dominance 87

6. Pleco Fez 108

7. The Nazi Method 128

8. Cerrito Blanco 148

The Deep Code

First time I ever met Stanley, my mother and I had pulled off the Interstate at a truck stop west of Missoula. We'd been living at this commune over in the Okanogan Valley, in Washington State. But then my mother wore out her welcome with the hippies, and we were back on the road again. It was three days to Ohio, and she said she needed a cold can of Hamm's and a Vick's nasal inhaler. This was in 1979. In those days such inhalers came with a ragged amphetamine in them. She'd cut the top off of the plastic. Then shove the little cotton swab down into a beer. Said she could drive all night like that. But then coming out of the store, she spied this little trucker bar up the road. Said she needed to get her mind right for the drive. So, we went back inside, where she bought me a *Savage Sword of Conan* and a meat stick. Then she dropped me off at the Gremlin. "Lock the doors," she said. "And don't talk to strangers."

    About an hour later, I'd read through that comic book twice. I was getting pretty bored, so I tucked it under my arm and hit the pavement. It was hot out there, late in the summer. I was standing around the parking lot with my hands shoved into my pockets. After life on the commune, I was feeling overwhelmed by all that concrete and diesel. It's been decades, now. But it still hits me sometimes, the whole Modern American thing. It's like some carnival sideshow. I get a little wiggy with it sometimes. Then

I've got to drop everything and head up The Bob, north of Missoula. I'll stay out there for a week in the wilderness, pretending the sideshow doesn't exist anymore. I'll get to thinking maybe there are no roads. No supermarkets or Chevron gas stations. Maybe the whole world is just wildflowers and mountain lakes. It's just me up there and the lumbering bears. I'm like a newborn child of some ancient goddess of the glaciers and the sunlight. I used to carry Stanley's old Smith and Wesson for the grizzlies, but I sold that piece last year after my mother died.

In 1979, though, I didn't know jack about bears. I was just another dumb kid, fresh off the commune, and I wasn't prepared for all that civilization, the cars and the RVs and the tractor-trailers. They came belching off the highway and up to the pumps. There was squawky music playing on the loud speaker, and Stanley, he was sitting on the curb, leaned up against the newspaper machine. If he had been a larger man, I might have been afraid of him. But he was small. Very thin and pale. He wore dirty jeans and sandals. He had these thick, polarizing sunglasses and a scraggly beard. He had a long, stringy wizard's tonsure growing from his head, and he'd unbuttoned his shirt to show off that pink flesh. He was like some kind of mollusk pulled out of the blackest gloom. He squinted at me. "King Thoth-Amon," he said, pointing at my comic book. "You ought to read the source novel: *Conan the Buccaneer*."

"I've read the first one," I said. I squatted on the concrete. He was a few years younger than my mother, who was pretty young to be the mother of a twelve-year-old boy. I unfolded the comic book. "And I've read *Conan of Cimmeria*, too."

"Ah, Bêlit," he said. He pointed at the cover. "She's from *Queen of the Black Coast*."

"It's a good story," I said. "If I lived in Conan's day, I'd be a pirate, too."

"There're still pirates in the world," he said. "Maybe you are a pirate. What's your name, kid?"

"Randal," I said. "But my mother told me not to talk to strangers."

"That's good advice," he said. "Your mother's a smart lady."

We could see her coming out of the trucker bar down the road, and we watched as she made her way through the parking lot. She looked kind of dodgy in her walk, all loose and wayward. She tripped over a chunk of concrete. When she got to us at the curb, she planted her hands on her hips. From the ground, Stanley gazed past her into the sky. He looked like a man about to take a mortar round straight out of the blue.

"Why are you talking to this strange man?" she said.

"My name's Dr. Stanley Sharpe," he said. He stood. He ran his fingers through his hair. "But you can call me Stanley. I've got a hibachi back at the RV, a couple burgers, and a six-pack of Hamm's. Why don't you come over and rest a bit?"

"We probably ought to be on the road," I said.

"You're a doctor?" she said. The wheels that were turning in her mind: a doctor equaled a prescription pad. "You know, I think a burger does sound pretty good right now."

She was dressed in cut-off jeans, my mother, and she had a T-shirt from the Indy-500. Her hair looked like the root-ball off a tree stump, but anybody could see she was out of Stanley's league. That's when I decided I didn't like him. I'd liked him for a minute. He was this guy I met out front of a truck stop, but then my mother walked up. I'd lost him. He wasn't even a medical doctor, either. Turned out he had a Ph.D. in systems theory from Stanford. Anyway, she'd had situations with a couple of the hippies back at the commune. Nothing serious, though. Not since my old man had killed himself. That was back in Ohio. He'd been selling financial products in the door-to-door market around Dayton when I was little. But they got heavy into drugs. LSD and speed. They'd go a week sometimes, blasted out of their minds. I was around eight in those days. I'd get hungry, I'd grab a book of food stamps out of the dresser, and buy a box of Lucky Charms at the corner store. That was life. But then he must've unwound that silver thread just a little too far. That's the thing about it. You want to roll on out there into the Aether. You want to get just a little bit further each time. Cut the bonds and glide with the cosmos. Weightless and serene. Just a little farther and then a little bit farther. It was this motel room, when he did it. There was a razor blade and a hot bath. I can still see the smudges of blood all down the side of the tub. In my dreams sometimes, I'm standing in that bathroom door. I'm dropping the Coca-Cola. My mother, she stands behind me. Her screams echo off the cinder block walls. I never could watch the *Mary Tyler Moore Show* again.

    My mother gave Stanley the keys to the Gremlin. He drove us down the road to this RV park called Paradise Place. It was full of Winnebagos, campervans, and teardrop trailers. The people all wore a lot of white slacks and geometric beige. We pulled up to his outfit, a '72 Town and Country with a shiny Airstream trailer on the hitch. He had a patio umbrella jabbed in the ground and a smoldering hibachi next to the stoop. He gestured up the steps, where we climbed into the trailer. There was a sink in there and a counter. He had a little stove and a refrigerator. It was a whole house, miniaturized. There was a couch down one side, a bed in the back, and on the table sat this computer. I'd never seen a computer before. It had a big keyboard, four floppy drives, and one of those hulking CRT monitors. On the screen, row upon row of green numbers flickered and danced. My mother popped her head back outside, suspicious suddenly of his intentions, his whole way of life.

    "It's an Apple II computer," he said.

    "It looks like financial data," she said. "My husband used to work with financial data."

    "You're married?" he said.

    "I'm divorced."

    I tell that same lie. It's what I tell Sheryl, my ex-wife. My parents were divorced, I say. My old man and me, we're estranged. I never hear from him. I told the headshrinker that same thing, too, the social worker, and the judge. I was still in the program when we had the hearing to decide on my visitation rights, and that lie was everybody's going theory. When you're in the program everybody needs a going theory to explain why you are the way you are, what your problem is, and why you need to pee in a cup before you can be allowed a few hours of supervised visitation with your only son. It was once a week in Sheryl's lawyer's office. They even made me pay for the damned cup. Came back negative, though, straight through the program without a scratch.

"If I show you something," said Stanley. "Do you promise you won't tell anybody?"

"Show me what?" my mother said.

"There's a code in the stock market," he said. "You've heard of Eliot Wave Theory? I'm pursuing certain ramification found deep within the Fibonacci Sequence."

My mother squinted at the monitor. "I don't believe in that crap," she said.

"It's true," he said. "Do you have any idea how much money can be made in derivatives contracts? I mean, if you know which way the market is going to swing?"

$$\theta$$

They were married for eight years, until Black Monday, October 19, 1987. That's when they crapped out. I'd heard he moved to Seattle, after that. Bought himself a sailboat. He was doing tours up the San Juans. He's in his sixties now. My mother, she died last year from liver failure. I used to wonder about him, too. So, maybe it would've been nice to see him again, but it was last Friday when he came by. Sheryl had brought Marty over for the afternoon. This was my first unsupervised visit since getting out of the program. She's doing okay, Sheryl. She's engaged to an orthodontist who advertises on the television. She's got that curly bob like all the soccer moms wear, but I can still see this barefoot girl, the one dancing in her motley skirt to that Grateful Dead cover band. I guess I always thought it would be like that forever.

It was after school when she pulled up to the house. Marty stayed in the car, while Sheryl marched to the porch in her pink capris and canvas topsiders. I knew what she was upset about. I do a little side-work on automobiles, so I had the engine wrestled out of a Ford Taurus in the front yard. I'd thrown a tarp over the hoist and the new engine, but there were parts laying in the dirt. I've got a couple of motorcycles, too, and my mother's old F-150. But it's the Gremlin that really bothered Sheryl. It's still out there, sitting on the rims, with lots of thistle growing up the doors. Marty used to like to play with the steering wheel and the gauges. He had a bunch of samurais and Luke Skywalkers he'd play with down on the floor. "There's battery acid," she said, "and broken glass. You told the judge you were getting rid of that thing."

"I've got a guy coming tomorrow," I said.

"I want this to work," she said. "But we've got to stick to the agreement."

"I'm all about the agreement," I said. "Had the social worker out here yesterday."

I'd scoured the house. There was no booze or drugs. I'd washed the dishes in the sink and scrubbed the bathrooms. I swept the linoleum and vacuumed out the carpets. I even re-organized my records, shuffling the Zeppelin behind the Stan Getz. I had been re-coning this set of Wharfdale speakers in the living room, and I had the drivers and the old cones scattered across the coffee table, but I told the social worker this was a father-son project. He seemed to like that. He marked it down on his clipboard. Meanwhile, I'd bought the supplies to make a couple of pizzas with Marty for dinner that evening.

"I'm on your side," she said. "You know that, right? You're the only one here who's not on your side."

Sheryl's father had been one of these corporate alcoholics. He'd worked himself into an early grave. I never met him, but even now I can see that she's looking at his ghost every time she looks at me. She'd pour herself into me if she could. If I'd only let her, she'd fill me up with herself. Then, maybe that old ghost might step right out. He'd wrap his arms around her. He'd tell her he loved her. But it just makes me angry. I used to tell her to go pour herself down some other drain. Then, I'd head out walking. I'd get up into the woods and try to stop thinking about everything all the time.

"I know you are," I said. "I'm glad you believe in me."

That seemed to please her, and she opened the car door. She reached across Marty for his book. It was just him, no backpack or duffle. We'd try a few hours this first time. In another month, we could talk to the judge about an overnight. But I didn't have to pee in a cup. There was no social worker. It was just me and Marty.

"I got Marty a cell phone," she said. "He has my number if there's a problem."

"There won't be a problem," I said. "We'll hang out. We'll make a couple of pizzas."

"That's your plan?" she said. "Hang out? Eat pizza?"

"Make pizza," I said. "Maybe we'll go for a hike up the Rattlesnake."

I've still got the three acres Stanley bought back in the '80s. I'm right at the end of the pavement. This dirt road winds up into the Rattlesnake Wilderness Area.

"Are you crazy?" she said. "He won't hike with you."

"Just up the Rattlesnake," I said.

Sheryl and I used to hike before the divorce. Marty, he's a good kid on a hike, too. But the last time we headed up The Bob together things got a little hairy. Our marriage was on the downhill slide. We were still wrestling with it, though, and we'd decided to give it another chance. We were on a five-day, and we were really going to try to be a couple again, a family. Sheryl had quit drinking, but I had this bottle of Canadian Hunter in my back-pack. It's good sipping around the fire at night. I used to like a little nip, just something to take the chill off the mountain while the sun goes down in the west.

 We'd struck out from the Benchmark trailhead early on the first day, crossed over the South Fork of the Sun River, and then hiked along the West Fork, up through the open prairie and the trees. We heard elk bugling in the morning, and on the second day, we saw a moose in a grove of aspen. There were bighorn sheep on the slopes and lots of quail in the fields along the water. By the third day, we'd hiked around Red Butte and then down to the Chinese Wall, this great overthrust of ancient rock winding through the heart of the wilderness. Mountain goats wander the ridges, eagles nest in the crags, and it's bear country out there, too. I've seen black bears along the banks of the little streams and in the meadows full of Indian paintbrush, stretching along the base of the scarp. And, of course, there are grizzlies in the Bob Marshall. I had never seen one, though, not in all my years of wandering in that country, not until we returned to camp that evening.

 We'd built a fire and eaten our soups out of the cans. I'd cracked open that bottle of Canadian Hunter, and we were sitting around listening to the flames. After a while we got to talking about the future. When you're on the skids, you don't talk much about the future. Out there in the woods, though, away from all the complications of our lives, it just seemed natural. I'm handy with cars, and there was this garage down the ass-end of Missoula on Brooks. They had a sign out hiring. Sheryl, she was talking about this two-year tech deal they've got up at the college. It was all kind of exciting, talking it out, the ideas flowing. We had that dome full of stars above us. There was a hot fire in a circle of stones at our feet. And I had a bottle of whiskey in my hands. Who knows what might have been, but it all hardened into resolve later that night when the bear came crashing through the shadows beyond the fire.

He was on us for five hours. It lasted all through the night. I'd polished off the bottle, and I had Stanley's Smith and Wesson. I kept staggering out toward the snuffled grunts. I was dragging this flaming branch, swinging arcs of fire into the blackness of the trees. The sparks rocketed into the void. I hurled the bottle into the bush. The fire twisted and curled at the end of my branch, and Sheryl kept yelling for me to shoot. She was crying and holding Marty. He was screaming, clawing at his mother, and in the gloom, I could see this giant shadow rise and fall. Sheryl's voice broke into jagged shards. I could hear it then, the pure rage she felt for me, the real hatred at my incompetence. In the darkness the trees split with the bear's feints. I fired off the pistol and that drove him back into the woods. But only for a time. I was firing wild. I was blind drunk with that pistol and I never did hit anything. We spent five hours like that, and it was the longest night I've ever spent in the woods.

And no, the Rattlesnake isn't the Bob Marshall. Still, it was just last spring that we had a grizzly come down here out of the Mission Mountains. That hasn't happened since the 1950s. Montana Fish and Wildlife say they tracked his radio collar right to the edge of town. I've seen bear digs out in the brush, and there are jagged claw marks on this pine up the road. They're wide apart as both of my hands can stretch.

"All right," I said. "We won't go hiking."

My evening with Marty, though, I think that would've gone okay. We played chess. We mixed the dough for the pizzas. We kneaded it onto the counter, and we set it back in the bowl to rise. Then we worked on the speakers. He was quiet, intent on the delicate cones. I showed him how to fit the spider onto the voice coil. I taught him how to spread the epoxy and how much to use. We were sitting on the couch together, working in silence. We had just finished one of the cones. That's when Stanley opened the front door. He still had his key from years ago. He just burst in. Right out of the blue. He stood framed in the doorway. He wore this offshore jacket and a thick pair of motorcycle boots. He was bald as an egg, now, with tattoos across the tops of his knuckles. When he grinned, I could see that he'd lost a couple of teeth. In his arms, like a baby, he cradled a case of Hamm's.

"You should've told me about your mother's funeral," he said.

"Hello, Stanley," I said. "This isn't really a good time."

He closed the door and set the beer on the coffee table. Grabbing two cans, he popped the tops and squatted on the floor. I tried to wave him off, but then I thought he might offer the beer to Marty, so, I took it. I held it. It had that nice film of condensation on the smooth aluminum.

"A good time would've been last year," he said. "When she actually died."

They had not split on amicable terms. It was Black Monday and I think possibly the whole country was in the process of getting divorced. You could hear the doors slamming all across America. The engines turning over. The tires squealing in the driveways. There were so many stereos hurled out of windows on that day. Pistols drawn. Pistols fired. In the great tapestry of that financial ruin, we were but a single thread, and though my mother never pulled the Smith and Wesson, she did keep it in her pocket, while he loaded his crap into the back of the U-Haul. Driving off, I heard him shout that eight years with us had been nine too many.

"I didn't think you'd want to come to the funeral," I said.

"Your mother and I had our problems," he said. "But that's water under the bridge."

"Then I suppose I'm sorry," I said. "I should've found you."

"I accept your apology," he said. "That why I brought you this peace offering."

"What do you mean a peace offering?" I said. I turned the beer around in my fingers.

"I'm moving back," he said.

"Back to Missoula?"

"Back to this house. It's my house, too. Don't you think?"

I set the beer down, but then I quickly picked it up again. "I don't believe a court of law would agree with you," I said.

"I don't want to talk about the law," he said. "I want to talk about the Fibonacci Sequence."

"Black Monday put an end to Eliot Wave Theory," I said. "We lost everything."

"Except for this house," he said. "And Eliot Wave Theory does work. We couldn't go deep enough with that Apple II, but I've got a new algorithm, now. I want to check it with the original data. Let it play out from '79 through Black Monday. See if it's predictive."

"What's Eliot Wave Theory?" said Marty.

"There's a deep code," said Stanley, "buried in the heart of the stock market."

"There's nothing to it," I said. "It's all voodoo."

"If you had unlimited wealth," he said, "what would you do with it?"

"I'd build a spaceship," said Marty.

"As we speak," he said, "there are tycoons building their own spaceships."

"Eliot Wave Theory is bunk," I said, "and we don't have anything to invest."

"We could sell this house," said Stanley.

I had the beer in my hand, and when he said that, I don't know, I just tipped the can to my mouth. All I did was, I let the beer touch my lips. I didn't drink it. I felt the pop of the carbonation. I smelled the wheat and the yeast. It's such a powerful smell. One of the greatest things in life, really. That first sip of beer. The one you take after a long, dry thirst.

θ

And I guess bears were on my mind again, after talking to Sheryl, but it wasn't that grizzly up the Bob Marshall or even the one that came through here last spring. It was the bear that Stanley had shot. That's what I remember most about that first night in the Airstream. It's not the Fibonacci Sequence or Eliot Wave Theory or the Apple II. It's that bear.

My mother had fallen asleep. She lay across the bed. I'd taken her shoes off and covered her with the blanket. The green numbers blinked on the monitor. Outside, the wind had begun to pull in the trees. I was standing in the doorway to the RV while Stanley fixed me a hamburger. He gave me a bag of Fritos, and he set me on the stoop with packets of catsup and mustard. Then he handed me a cold can of Hamm's. I almost didn't take it. I was a kid, and I didn't drink beer. But then I did take it, and I felt older for doing so. That was my first dead soldier, too. Right there in that Airstream.

After I ate, Stanley showed me the computer. He cleared the numbers off the screen, and we wrote a simple program in BASIC to print my name in staggered, diagonal columns. He dug out a floppy disk and stuck it into one of the drives. It was that old headshrinker program, *Eliza*. It's a simple feedback loop of questions and answers, the most rudimentary of natural language processors, nothing like todays AIs, but I'd never seen anything like it, a kind of living mind. Then, he showed me *Taipan!* and *Pyramid*, *Apple Writer* and *VisiCalc*. He showed me the numbers, too, the graphs, and the Fibonacci Sequence. On the back of a napkin, he drew a spiral. It was like the shell of a chambered nautilus. He drew the arms of a galaxy. The Golden Section, he called it. These are the numbers that govern the phyllotaxic spirals of the daisy, the sunflower, he said. They govern the structure of the pine cone and the curve of a sheep's horn. "The vortices of a flowing cloud are written in these numbers," he said, "and so is the mind of man. All his hopes and fears and desires. Everything that he will ever build and create and destroy. Your mind and your soul and all there is about you. These are but the epiphenomena of a deep code that lies buried in the heart of reality."

"And you know the code?" I said.

"Once you know the code," he said, "then you have awakened. You are no longer of this world. You are a being of light, and to you, all things have become known."

We'd been at the computer for a couple hours when my mother finally rolled to her back. She sat up in bed. It was evening coming on. Stanley sat cross-legged on the blanket. He took a wooden box from beneath his bed, and from the box, he drew a pack of zig-zags and a baggie full of weed. He rolled a joint and licked it, and he twisted the ends. This he handed to my mother. I had begun to find it all rather irritating, too. We'd been having a good time, me and Stanley. But now they were going to do adult things. Probably, I'd have to wait outside. She took a drag off the joint, coughed, and lost the hit, which I guess meant it was harsh stuff. In retrospect that's where my skepticism should've kicked it. Guy thinks he's one of the illuminated, but he doesn't even have a line on some decent weed.

"Here's ten dollars," he said. "Why don't you two go grab us some more beer."

My mother and I walked the quarter mile to the truck stop, where we picked up two six-packs of Hamm's. It was cool out, and the tractor-trailers moaned along the highway in the mountains. Dead grass blew in the fields and across the low hills. There were little patches of sage and thistle. All these big stones had been carried down by the glaciers long ago. There weren't many trees, to speak of. Only a few knobby pines grew along the road. That's where we saw the black bear. He was up one of those pines. I'd never seen a bear, not out in the open like that. He was ten feet up the trunk, swaying from side to side. We were walking into the wind, blinking at the dust as we passed beneath the tree. I was struck dumb by the sight of him. The terror of it. There he was, staring down at me, this incredible bear. I dropped the six-pack, and it burst on the pavement. The cans rolled and scattered. A few cracked their seals, spewing arcs of beer across the dirt. I was mesmerized, rooted to the earth.

"Get back to the trailer," my mother whispered. "And pick up those beers."

At the trailer, Stanley had built a fire in the pit. Flames licked the sky, and sparks burst and flew in the night. I sat cross-legged on the steps and picked up my *Conan*, which I began to read by the golden light. They popped a couple of beers, and she told him about the bear. It was maybe ten minutes that passed. They'd shotgunned a joint and killed those Hamm's. Stanley had been talking about the options market, but then my mother must've mentioned the bear again. She was pretty shook up about it. She couldn't get those eyes out of her head. That's when Stanley jumped. I was startled and I dropped my comic book into the fire, and I can still see the pages roaring in that burst of green flame. I grabbed after it, but it was gone. Stanley ducked into the Airstream. When he came back, he had the Smith and Wesson. He'd cracked the cylinder, and he was loading cartridges into the chambers. "No woman of mine need fear the night," he said. It was something Conan would've said. He's about five foot three, but a Smith and Wesson will make a Conan out of anybody.

He stuffed the pistol into the waistband of his pants, and he charged through the RVs, out toward the road. I trailed behind him, running to keep up. My mother, she kept calling out for us to stop. Get back to the trailer. But I wouldn't listen. I followed him down to that knobby pine, where the bear still clung to the tree. And maybe he was about to drop to the ground. I guess he might've charged. I don't know. They seem to lumber, bears, but they'll charge with amazing speed. He was clawing chunks out of the bark. I watched his muscles ripple beneath the fur. When my mother caught up to us, we all stood looking up the trunk. Then I heard this low, breathy wail. It was the first time in my life that I had ever heard that sound, those pulsed and broken grunts. Stanley raised the pistol. He fired and the bear let out this pitiful squeal. It fell into the road, and when it tried to get up, Stanley fired again. There was silence after that, pure silence. It rolled through the fields and the little hills. It went all the way down the road and out into the valleys and along the rivers. I had begun to cry. I was a twelve-year-old boy, and I was pretty maudlin about such things. I'd been reading that Conan, too. Thinking about the bear. I'd been wondering, you know, what if he was my bear? It came to me in this flash of brain light. I could've ridden that bear into the woods. I could've lived with him in a cave down by the stream. Maybe I'd have grown up one day to be the King of the Night Glade. I'm prone to fits like that. Melancholy drama, and maybe that's what went wrong with Sheryl and me. It's just that I can't stop thinking that something magical is about to happen. It's like this whole pasteboard carnival sideshow might suddenly vanish one day, and then I'll find myself alive again, living in the deep green of some ancient order of gods and truth and justice. Some fairy-book land beyond the prison of space and time.

"Let's get out of here," said Stanley. "Before someone sees us."

They headed along the road, back to the RV. But I didn't follow them. Instead, I wandered into the field. I walked through the charging grass and the wind. I could hear them calling after me, but I didn't want to be around them anymore. And I started to run. I thought maybe they'd chase me. They sounded pretty angry, like this was all my fault somehow. And I got far away from the road, out staggering in the rocks and the weeds. I walked in circles through the dirt. And I guess they finally gave up on me. I sat in the grass. I lay on my back. I looked into the stars, and I wondered what it would be like to simply melt into the earth, to lie like that forever, and to sprout weeds from my flesh and bones. And sometimes I think that I never got up from the field. I've been there this whole time, with those stars still pouring down my cheeks. I can see the black fields in a night that goes on forever. And so perhaps it was only a ghost of me that went slouching back to the Airstream. All these decades later, I'm just a ghost, wandering through the ephemera of someone else's middle age.

I never told Sheryl about that. Just like I never told her about my old man. And I guess it's too late to tell her now. She'd only pity me, the way she does. She'd make me go see the shrink again, too. But it's nothing any shrink can fix. A shrink's nothing more than *Eliza*, that old dead program. They're like the high priests of the market place. But sleep is all they sell. They have no power to split the sky.

θ

Down in the basement I've got this pile of obsolete electronics, old TVs, VCRs, and computers. I've got about a dozen different systems. Towers and laptops. I've got dead monitors and old printers. I've got a box full hard drives, bags of memory chips and sound cards. Controllers and motherboards lay scattered across the floor. It's all twisted together in a jumble of cables and mice and keyboards. There's a couple of interesting relics, too. Machines out of the Golden Age. I've got a Commodore 64. I've got an Osbourne One. It's this portable that looks like a suitcase nuke. And I've still got Stanley's original Apple II. I've got his floppy disks and all the data.

We'd gone to the basement, so that Stanley could find it and run it through his new algorithm. He had a laptop with him and Kryoflux USB floppy controller. Said he could use that to load a raw dump off the disks into an Apple II emulator on his laptop. He just had to get the drives to spin up. I figured if I gave him the drives and the disks, maybe he'd leave. Get a motel room. Just so he wasn't here when Sheryl came back.

Stanley had found the monitor. Marty sat on a box of dot-matrix printout with a flashlight. He was reading the labels off a bunch of floppies. Somehow, I had this fresh beer in my hand. I think probably it was my second, though it might have been my third. They were still talking about spaceships and the feasibility of asteroid mining, the impact on the world economy of two billion tons of iron ore. I found it irritating, their whole conversation. Not because it isn't interesting. I'd have gotten around to talking about asteroid mining, but then Stanley pops up. It's like he rode in on a meteor. He's this demon of dreams. But his dreams are all fire and steel, power and wealth. He's got lasers for eyes. I could see he was burning right through Marty. He was cutting him straight down to the bones.

I said, "You ever think about that bear?"

"What bear?" said Stanley.

"The one you shot out of the tree."

"You shot a bear?" said Marty. It was the way Marty said it. The admiration in his voice sent this shock through me. Anger that split my chest. Stanley set down the monitor. He found the keyboard beneath the disk drives. They were still daisy-chained together with ribbon cable. I set my beer on top of a stack of tape decks and picked up this CD player. Bits of plastic rattled inside the case. I kicked over a pile of Betamax tapes and laserdiscs.

"I never shot any bear," said Stanley.

"You did," I said.

"Well, I don't want to talk about bears," he said.

"Why'd you shoot a bear?" said Marty.

"That never happened," said Stanley. He was squatting, digging at the dirty grime caked on the monitor screen. He rubbed his thumb over it. "Bears ought not to come around people."

"Here it is," said Marty, he held up a package of floppy disks. "August, 1979."

"All right, kid," said Stanley. "Let's go make a fortune."

"You shouldn't be here," I said. "I want you to go."

It was dark in the basement. The air felt cool, and I pulled the cord on the bulb. A hard, white light jumped around the piles of junk. In the oscillation, our shadows grew and retreated along the walls. I was gripping the banister. I had that can of Hamm's. Marty held the box of floppies. He was watching me, and I had begun to cry. I was shaking with the tears, and I don't think I'd really had that much to drink, even. People keep saying that I was drunk. But I'd only had one or maybe two beers. I was lucid. In fact, I don't know that I have ever been so lucid in all of my life. It was hatred and rage. That's all it was. I saw the whole basement suddenly, charged in this shimmer. It came bursting up my spine. This jarring shock. It felt like I'd hit my funny bone, but it was all over me. And I hurled that beer and bonged it off Stanley's eye. He just sat down hard in the junk. Marty let out a gasp, and Stanley grabbed the side of his face. There was this long, slow groan. I wanted to know what I'd done, so I knelt to pull his hand away. He was cursing me, and he didn't want me to touch him, but he was pretty old now, and he wore down quick. I wrestled him to the concrete. I pinned his arms. Marty was jumping all over the place. He kept hollering for me to quit it, to let him up. But I thought maybe I'd knocked his eye out, and I wanted to see that for myself, not hear it second hand. I wanted to see the eyeball, like a little onion. I wanted it hanging there out of the socket.

Sadly, I hadn't even broken the skin. He was going to have a nice sized lump, though. Maybe his eye would even swell shut. But he wasn't going to be permanently maimed. Guys like Stanley, they never are. I took him under the armpits. "Help me get him up the steps," I said.

Marty took his feet, and it was then that I noticed he was crying, too. Together we dragged him up the stairs from the basement. Stanley tried to protest, but mainly he just complained about his diskettes.

"What's the matter?" I said.

"You hit me in the eye," he said.

"I'm talking to Marty," I said. "What's wrong?"

Marty looked at me sideways. He helped me plop him onto the couch. Then, he went back to the basement to bring up the disk drives and the floppies. In the kitchen, I filled a baggie with ice. I took it to the couch and laid it across Stanley's face. He gave me this withering look and tried to push it away. "Calm down," I said. "This isn't a big deal."

However, I was beginning to see that it was kind of a big deal. I mean, it seems like a small thing. You whack a guy in the head with a beer. I've been whacked in the head with beers. Worse than beers. Sheryl whacked me in the head one time with a ceramic bong. No big deal. But then the music stopped and I was the last one standing. So, when I whacked a guy in the head with a beer, suddenly it was this big deal. The bigness of it was growing, too. Compounding. There's a smooth, uniform surface to life. Maybe it's blistered with small dazzles of pleasure or pain. But then there are great ruptures, too, titanic shifts that forever alter the orbits. My mother had died from liver failure. I had gotten myself divorced. Stanley had shot a bear. Then there's my old man. He just couldn't take it anymore, and he'd opened up his veins. I could see it was all happening again. My old life was falling away. Here was this new life coming into existence. Truncated and diminished. I'd walked another turn of the screw, but all I'd found down here was another level of the maze.

That's when Sheryl's car pulled into the yard. I watched her walk through the junkers and up to the door. She hadn't liked the presence of a new car, I could tell. And she liked even less the strange old man laid out on the couch. She folded her arms across her chest, taking in the scene.

The glow of the late afternoon filled the sky, and the dead grass of the fading summer drifted through the yard. I knelt with the ice pack against Stanley's head. There might've been an explanation for this. Maybe he was a neighbor. He'd had a wreck. The curtains billowed in the windows, and the wind blew Sheryl's hair.

"You sure clocked him," said Marty. He set the drives on the coffee table, next to Stanley's laptop and piled the diskettes next to them. Stanley groaned on the couch. I had the baggie full of ice, and there were a couple of warm Hamm's sitting on the floor. She took it all in.

"You hit this man?" she said.

"With a can of beer," said Marty. "I'm amazed he's not dead."

"You can't kill somebody with a can of beer," I said.

"Then you wrestled me down," said Stanley. "You tried to gouge my eye out."

"I did not try to gouge your eye out."

"You hit him with a beer?" said Sheryl. "Then you wrestled him to the floor. This old man?"

"I ought to press charges," said Stanley.

"This isn't the first time you've been whacked in the head with a beer," I said.

"It was cute once," said Sheryl. She held the sides of her temples. "You know that? All your crazy shit. But that was long ago."

She knelt beside me at the couch to see what damage I had done. She smelled of lavender and sage, and it made me think of all those wildflowers in the meadows up the Bob. She'd had this frame pack that loomed over her head, and she was such a trooper. She never once bitched about the forty pounds of gear. Stanley had a growing knot on the side of his face, about the size of a golf ball. She held his eyelid open, and I could see that a few capillaries had burst in the white.

"It wasn't a full can," I said.

"I really do want Marty to have a father," she said. "But this is what happens."

"It's nothing," I said.

"What's the matter with you?" she said. "What is it that makes you like this? You have a simple task. Be a normal father for a few hours. Make a pizza with your son. There are millions of fathers all over the world who are doing this with their sons. Why can't you be one of them? It's just a few hours on a Friday evening."

She used to ask me questions like that a lot when we were married. And every time she asked, I was always blasted back to that motel room. I even came close to telling her this one time. I'd gotten suspended from school, I told her. And we had decided to go down to this amusement park, near Cincinnati. My old man, he really hated those rides. He was afraid of the coasters and the lines made him angry, but my mother talked him into it. He'd been pissed all day, though. Yelling at me. Yelling at my mother. He yelled at everybody he could see to yell at. You're getting catsup on your shirt. Sit still. Get over here. When we got back to the motel room, he had this beer in his hand. He just threw it against the wall, and it spattered out flat like a bug. That's when my mother left. She just turned and walked right out the door. There I was, standing in the motel room. I had my hands in my pockets. I told that to Sheryl. She listened. I got right down to the end of it. I was just standing there. Sheryl, she was patient with me. Had to be. But she was like, yeah, so what?

I never could tell her about the long, dead look, he gave me. The way he made me feel like a carcass. Some husk. I think maybe I was a phase he'd gone through, a kind of shell from something that's crawled off and left. He said to watch the TV. He said he needed a bath. But when he got to the door, he turned. It was this one last time. He looked back at me and he said, "Don't ever have children, Randal." That's the last thing he ever said. I sat on the edge of the bed, listening while he filled the tub. Then, I heard him sink down in the water. I heard it splash over the side. The afternoon turned into the evening. Eventually my mother came back, and she had a couple of Coca-Colas with her. We were getting hungry, too. But he never came out, and when we finally opened the door, what I remember most were those red smudges from his fingers. They went down the side of the tub. It was like he'd tried to stand at one point. Maybe he'd changed his mind. But he couldn't get under his own weight. His body lay submerged in the red water. Only his arm lay on the side of the tub, with a long, jagged gash up the middle of his wrist. It was that *Mary Tyler Moore Show* on the television behind me.

Sheryl said, "I've spent the last fifteen years of my life asking you what your problem is."

"This is Stanley," I said. "He shot a bear. I was Marty's age. I was twelve."

"He shot a bear?" she said. "You and your goddamned bears."

"You nearly put my eye out on account of some bear?" said Stanley.

"Get your things," she said. She took a finally accounting of the scene.

"Next week will be different," I said.

"What makes you think there's going to be a next week?"

Marty used to climb these trees. He'd get way up there. Then he wouldn't know how to get down. It was that same bewildered expression on his face, that longing. But there was something solidifying in his features now. The old longing flickered for an instant, like a shape caught in the lightning. But then the darkness fell around him and he was gone. Everything had shifted with Marty. I called his name, but he wouldn't look at me anymore. He scanned the room for his book. Then he walked out the screen. He let it slam shut behind him, and he stomped through the yard to Sheryl's car, where he flung first his book and then himself into the backseat. And so, I guess it's over with us now. I don't mean that I'll never see him again, but it's going to be in this certain way. There are sons who hug their fathers when they say goodbye, and there are others that only shake their hands. A kind of murky haze has come between them.

"I won't make him see you," she said. "He gets to decide for himself now."

After she had left, I walked out to the porch, then down into the yard and through the junkers. Stanley kept calling to me from the door. He said he was going to fire up the drives and run the numbers. Didn't I want to watch? We could have a Hamm's. And where was that old pistol, anyway? The Smith and Wesson? I ignored him. Maybe if I closed my eyes hard enough he'd simply blink out of existence. I drifted along the pines that divide us from our neighbors. I squatted in the road. I looked up the Rattlesnake. In the summertime the sun stays out forever in these mountains, and it was that late evening light in the sky. I could smell the sap and the wildflowers. He called out again, and I started walking, like I just meant to walk on forever. There are meadows up there, and I could sleep on beds of pine duff. Let him have the damned house. His dreams. The Deep Code. He's right, of course. It does belong to him. I didn't steal it. He did. And I could build me a lean-to out of fallen branches. I could lash it together with ropes made of fire weed and thistles.

I was still thinking about Marty and Sheryl, my father, and what he said in the motel room. He never would've been so irritated at the amusement park if I hadn't gotten myself suspended from school. That's where it starts for me. From there my mind is like a revolving door. Around and around it goes. It's an endless carnival ride. I'm in the doorway. I'm dropping the Coca-Cola. There are red smudges of blood down the side of the tub. *Mary Tyler Moore* plays on the TV. My mother shrieks and the beer explodes and the lines at the rides were so long that day. Don't ever have children, he said, and I've always thought that he must have hated me in that moment. But now I'm not so sure. He had decided. He knew what he was about to do. He had turned away. He was releasing himself from all of the suffering that we endure. So, perhaps it wasn't hate that he was feeling at all, but rather love. Maybe he just didn't want me to have to go through that same kind of pain. He wanted it to be easy for me when I made the decision to finally let it all go. Yes. I think in that one moment that was his way of saying that he loved me.

This is the untouchable thing that lies coiled in the pit of my heart.

I was about a hundred yards up the road. I'd wandered past a bunch of timbers that had fallen into a draw. There're lots of little channels in the earth up there, where the deer have carved their quiet and careful paths. Brown needles cover the forest ground. Wind rustled in the trees. It was that pine out there by the road that I came to, the one with the slash marks down the side. That wound was rust colored now and full of hard sap. The grizzly from last spring, his prints had washed away in the rain, but I could still see where he had forced the twigs aside. What a great, loping shadow he must've been, disappearing into the gloom of the far trees. I placed my hands together on the trunk of the pine, and it was only by this doubling that I could span the width of his paw. I called out to him. I yelled up the road. I called out again and again for him to come and find me. Come take me home. Let's go up to that cave in the deep roots of the rolling hills. But all I ever heard back was the silence that follows a man's voice in the woods.

The Golden Horde of Mississippi

All that long morning of her cousin Bobby's funeral, Jessica Sue had meant to tell Grandma Lucy about the Golden Horde of Mississippi, but as usual they were fighting and the music video hadn't come up. To be fair, Jessica Sue was wearing a ratty pair of Dickies jeans and a faded Megadeth T-shirt. She knew perfectly well that wasn't proper funeral attire. But she hadn't come to visit expecting Bobby to slide his Harley-Davidson up under that eighteen-wheeler. Anyway, this was how Bobby would've wanted her to dress, and it was his funeral. Wasn't he the one cremated and packed into that lavender and gold cloisonné urn up there on the mantelpiece?

Eye-level with the urn, she could picture his nasty little eyes floating around in there with a few pieces of bone and patches of charred flesh in the otherwise uniform ash of a human being. She could tell you from the classes she was taking at the university that when you boil him all down to gravy there's perhaps a dollar's worth of chemicals in a human being. If you unfold his organs down to their proteins and his proteins down to their amino acids and his amino acids down to their constituent elements, you're not left with much to bargain on. The magic, she thought, and the wonder are all in the folds. And folded within each of the billions upon billions of cells that make up a human body there is over six feet of DNA.

Six feet. But here in this urn was Bobby, unfolded, brought by fire down to his basic state. And yet, thinking of her cousin Jessica Sue couldn't help but wonder, were there chunks of him in there that had simply refused to go peacefully?

"My Bobby was a good boy," said Grandma Lucy. "He'd want you in a black dress, and he'd want your hair combed like a nice young lady."

Bobby had been a lot of things, but "good boy," never had been one of them. Not even Grandma Lucy, who could see the good in a tornado—Grandma Lucy lived for a tornado—not even Grandma Lucy had ever called him a good boy when he was alive. "Bobby was a little freak," said Jessica Sue, maybe louder and more emphatic than she'd meant to.

"Well, he never once talked back to me," she said. "And he came over all the time to check on me and to mow my yard and to clean the gutters and to take the trash out. He took care of his grandmother, like a good child."

That had set Jessica Sue to fuming. She drove in silence up Mendenhall Road to the church, while Grandma Lucy, with the lavender cloisonné urn clutched to her chest, rattled off the litany of her misfortune. How could her own children have grown up to abandon such monsters as these, her grandchildren, into her care? Why had she sent Jessica Sue off to college? All the girl had learned down at Southern was to disrespect her elders, to deny the existence of God, and to go around wearing not even a stitch of underwear in a ratty pair of Dickies and a T-shirt with pictures of the Devil on it. That's why Jessica Sue hadn't gotten around to talking about the video.

The night before the funeral, she and her cousin-in-law Shauna, Bobby's widow, had sat up until three in the morning at the Waffle House plotting it out. They'd video the band playing in the sanctuary and then the service. They'd splice it all together with home movies of Bobby as a child and whatever weird stop-action stuff they could find off the internet: flowers growing in seconds, the spinning dome of the stars above. Cosmic. That was the vibe they were going for, and by the time they were done working it out, she really thought they'd managed to capture the spiritual essence of just who Bobby was. Of just what Bobby stood for. And when they parted ways, she told Shauna not to worry, to just get the Horde out to the church early and set up. She said she'd have Grandma Lucy well in hand by the time they got there. "Just tell Reverend Duey it was Grandma Lucy's idea," she said. "He's scared shitless of Grandma Lucy."

But then they fought, and she hadn't said a thing all morning. Truth be told, she'd lost a good bit of the reckless abandon of the night before, and she was a little nervous as they pulled into the parking lot at First Methodist of Lidell, where she saw it all spilled out and reeling across the asphalt and the flowerbeds. There were a dozen Harley-Davidson motorcycles, little demons of steel and leather. One had a sidecar. Another was a chopper with six-foot chrome forks. There was a jacked-up Malibu, and a ragged-out Econoline van. Painted black with house paint, the words, GOLDEN HORDE OF MISSISSIPPI, had been slashed across the side in dripping red. Parked in the handicapped zone was Shauna's brother's trike. Made from the back-half of a Volkswagen Beetle, its doors were decorated with pictures of stacked skulls and crawling rats. This round gut of a man, all sunglasses and hair, sat revving the motor, slow and methodical, just to hear the blast. In the flowerbed by the front steps of the church, these latter-day Tamerlanes had planted their standard, a six-foot weight bar sharpened to a point like a spear and festooned about the top with black horsetails falling around the hubcap off a '59 Edsel. Welded to a crossbar and painted gold were the letters GAM, which Bobby claimed was Latin. "Fucking Latin," he'd told her. "Like fucking ancient Rome. *Grex Aurum Mississippae*, motherfucker." A necklace of cat skulls hung around the hubcap. It was something Bobby used to wear over his pale and emaciated chest whenever he sang.

Little knots of people milled about the parking lot, greeting and shaking hands. They were big men, most of them older than Bobby, in T-shirts, faded denim, biker leather and thick-soled boots. The women with them looked hard, in stiletto heels and leopard print, Metallica and Iron Maiden T-shirts. All around the parking lot slouched these masses of greasy hair and dark bloodshot eyes. There were missing limbs and twisted faces, scarred with broken teeth. They were gathering towards the church, all pressing in towards the doors. These were Bobby's people, his friends, the members of his band. At the corners of the parking lot, a few groups of family clung to one another, making their way slowly or not at all. Some stood in bewilderment. Others had gotten back into their cars to leave.

"That Godforsaken little tramp," said Grandma Lucy. "Where is that slut?"

Jessica Sue traced her finger along the necklace of cat skulls. She thought of Bobby in the garage screaming into a microphone. "Come on," she said. Grandma Lucy had the urn cradled to her chest like a football, so Jessica Sue couldn't get her arm, but she took the old woman's elbow and led her up the steps and into the sanctuary. They found Shauna at the altar, dragging an electrical cord along the baseboards. Her bleach-blonde hair was done up like the top end of a pineapple. Commotion was general in the church. Two groups of bikers were attempting to erect klieg lights at either side of the altar. A couple of other men had video cameras. They argued about angles and shadow, while a Klingon warrior wandered through the sanctuary with a light meter. The Horde's lead guitarist—one of Bobby's co-workers at the Jiffy Lube in Lidell—stood in front of a Marshall stack playing with feedback.

"What in God's name?" said Grandma Lucy. "Where's Reverend Pickett?"

"Reverend Duey," Jessica Sue reminded her.

The Mintons had been members of First Methodist of Lidell for over fifty years. Ever since Grandpa come home from the war with that great splash of color across his chest, and told her he'd found Christ in a foxhole on Guadalcanal. Leastwise that's the way Grandma Lucy told it. There were bombs going off all around his head. Japs charged out of the darkness. And there he was down in that mud pit with nothing but a busted shovelhead and a Bible. Grandpa never talked much about it. Truthfully, he just never talked. But Grandma Lucy could talk the horns off a goat. She said, when the Light come on him in the darkness of that foxhole, he just stood up right where he was. He walked out and took to killing Japs left and right with that busted shovelhead. Sent them on down to hell, she said. And through these tales Jessica Sue and Bobby had grown up with this image of Grandpa in their heads. He was miles tall, walking his way along the ring of fire. He hopped from island to island, as though across stepping-stones, and he sowed the land with atom bombs, laying them down like he carried them in a sack, a kind of Johnny Appleseed of nuclear death. "Atom Bomb," Grandma Lucy used to say. She'd smile, her eyes twinkling bright. If there was one thing Grandma Lucy loved besides her grandbabies, Jesus and a good tornado, it was the atom bomb. And that's how come the Mintons were Christians, she said. It was to thank Jesus for seeing Grandpa home from the war and also for sending our great nation the bomb. After the war, she had sewed his medals into a square of black velvet, which she had embroidered on either side with the images of Douglas Macarthur and Robert E. Lee. This she hung on the wall over the mantelpiece, between a painting of Jesus and several pieces of Elvis Presley commemorative flatware, the ones with him in that shiny gold suit. It was the perfect shrine for Grandpa's pewter urn full of ashes, which now sat before his medals on a beautiful lace doily, just like Grandma Lucy had planned it.

    At First Methodist, there were Mintons everywhere. They sat on all the committees. They taught Sunday school classes. And they sang in the church choir. It was Grandma Lucy's sister who played the organ.

And in all those years it'd been Reverend Pickett up at the pulpit. He was one of these godly men who had been born old, with the soft and pliant skin of the sunless. His sermons were as regular as a metronome, and Grandma Lucy insisted he was the wisest man she'd ever met. Of course, Jessica Sue thought him a fool. They'd bickered about that for years, but it was pointless now. Reverend Pickett had died that spring of a coronary embolism. Reverend Duey had been with the church for seven months now, and the changes had not been to Grandma Lucy's liking. Reverend Duey must've been about thirty years old. He was full of passion and vigor for the Lord, and his righteousness had a tendency to manifest itself in spontaneous song and guitar plunking. He was earnest to a fault, and he drove Grandma Lucy nuts saying things like, "People have to find their own path to Jesus," and "The Lord works in mysterious ways."

"Reverend Duey," said Grandma Lucy. The revulsion rolled around in her mouth.

Shauna yelled to them from the altar. "Ya'll done brought Bobby. Good. Hey, everybody, Bobby's here, we can get rolling." She flopped the electrical cord over the pulpit and bounced down the aisle. "Ain't it just great?" she said. "I ain't slept a wink all night. Soon as we left the Waffle House, I got the Horde all woke up and told 'em. We're almost ready to go. But ya'll know where there's an electrical socket?"

"There's one by the choir box," said Jessica Sue.

"Where is Duey?" said Grandma Lucy.

"What are you plugging in?" said Jessica Sue. "I guess I envisioned something a little simpler, a camcorder maybe. Where'd you get the lights?"

"Duey!" Grandma Lucy screamed. "Reverend, you best get out here quick."

"They's a junior high up the road there," said Shauna. "My brother'll put 'em back when we're done. Look, I got to plug in Bobby's microphone."

Jessica Sue looked at the urn.

"Duey! Reverend!"

Reverend Duey stuck his head out from the back door. He had a slightly crazed look about him, his hair electric, his tie askew. He came hurriedly down the aisle to meet them. "Now, this is all just fine here," he said. "Everything is under control."

"Under control?" said Grandma Lucy. "This place is run amok with hoodlums."

"What's Bobby need a microphone for?"

"It is under control, Mrs. Minton," said Duey. "They're different folks. That they are. But they're the children of the Lord, too. And they've been very professional."

"What's he need it for?" said Shauna, utterly dismayed. "To sing 'The Dirge Of The Dark Sun,' liked we talked about at the Waffle House."

"I remember," said Jessica Sue. "But can't it just look like he's got a microphone?"

Grandma Lucy sniffed the air. Jessica Sue had noticed the faint odor of marijuana when they first came into the church, and she'd been hoping Grandma Lucy wouldn't smell it. "Reverend Duey," she said. "This here is a house of God, for Christ's sake."

"It's that Dark Star," said Shauna. "Bobby was obsessed with it. You know what he said? It was right before he got on that motorbike and headed for Biloxi. He said, it was the Dark Star that was ultimately real, not nothing else. And he said to sing the Dirge, you got to sing it real."

"As Jesus tells us," said Reverend Duey. "My father's house has many rooms, Mrs. Minton. Now, Bobby was a different boy, you know? But the Lord comes to folks like Bobby too."

"I see," said Jessica Sue. "Since the Dark Star isn't a metaphor, you can't have just the metaphor of a live mike? That's what you're saying. You've got to have the real live mike even for the video?" Shauna wrinkled up her nose. She put her hands to her hips and a couple of creases formed across her forehead.

"Different?" said Grandma Lucy. "There weren't nothing different about my Bobby. He was a good boy."

"Well," said Shauna, her enthusiasm on the wane. "I don't reckon I know nothing about no metaphors. I just know Bobby said it was ultimately real is all."

"He was a good boy," said Reverend Duey. "But he was a dog with a different set of fleas. He's in a better place now, Mrs. Minton. He sings with the angels. But we're all still here to carry on. And these are Bobby's people. They want to remember him in this way."

"Yes," said Jessica Sue. She jumped to her toes as she spoke. "Yes, you see, Shauna, the Dark Star is ultimately real. All this time I've been thinking of it as just a metaphor. I was thinking it was like maybe a symbol for Bobby's social estrangement. But it's not just a metaphor. It's for real. I mean theoretically, anyway. So what Bobby was saying is that it's an ultimately real metaphor. You see?"

Shauna looked around. "I just need to plug his mike in," she said. "So's he can sing the song."

"His people?" said Grandma Lucy. "His people? This trash ain't his people. Look at them."

"Shauna here was his wife," said Reverend Duey. He was kind of backing up as he said it, like maybe he'd be able to back all the way up past the morning and beyond last night and over the previous week to a world where Bobby hadn't slammed his Harley-Davidson under that semi-trailer. Perhaps there was a world out there with no Mintons in it at all. Just shiny, proper Methodists all lined up and ready to do good things and be good people. Shauna must've really laid into him this morning when she sprung it on him.

"I am his Grandmother," said Grandma Lucy. She placed one hand over her heart and tucked the urn into the crook of her elbow.

"I raised him myself. I raised up a half-dozen children, Reverend Duey. Some were mine, and some weren't, like Bobby and Jessica Sue here, whose own fathers done left out on them. I raised every last child the Lord seen fit to send me, and every last one of them was a good little boy or girl. You can believe that. And let me tell you something else. There ain't going to be no devil music at my Bobby's funeral. The sheriff won't have any truck with it. And don't you think I won't call him. I got my cellular telephone."

They were all dead silent after that. All the murmurs drew to a close. Even the footfalls ceased, and all eyes in the room focused on the group of them standing in the aisle. The Golden Horde had all spent nights in jail. Some had done ninety days. Jessica Sue knew for a fact Shauna's brother had done twelve months. They were the sort who lived their lives watching in the rearview mirror. When they looked through their peepholes to the unexpected knock at the door, it wasn't a vision of thugs come to rob them that flashed through their heads, but sheriff's deputies. There might have been a slight churn of violence in the sweat-filled air of the church sanctuary. But it died in the thoughts of flashing strobe lights and squad cars. It was as if, spewed from Grandma Lucy's mouth, the deputies themselves had come boiling into the room, swinging their batons and cocking their shotguns. The whole crowd seemed to heave as one, then to sink into the pews. Grandma Lucy looked upon them with disdain. Reverend Duey tried to wipe the startled look off his face. But he only managed to blur himself into a long O of panic and uncertainty as he saw his ministry evaporating. Shauna dropped the microphone. The Golden Horde seemed to deflate as one, and there was only dead silence in the church.

It might've ended that way. But as Grandma Lucy always maintained, she was prone to argument, and Jessica Sue just couldn't get past the difference that had come over Bobby in this last year of his life. It wasn't that Bobby had been a lazy child. On the contrary he'd always hurled himself full force into whatever weirdness had captivated his infernal brain. Typically, his interests had tended toward the destructive, not the creative. He'd built zip guns and sparkler bombs. Under his mattress—where a normal boy might keep a swiped copy of Playboy—Bobby had hidden his intricately detailed designs for a homemade nuclear device. Yet he had not managed to pass high school science. Nor for that matter had he managed to pass high school. He could spill out endlessly on the great crimes and psychopaths of world history, such that the banks of the Oxus River were more real to him than the state of Mississippi. It was as if he too had come raging off the steppes to lay waste to the fatted children of the valleys. "To carry off their daughters," he'd scream at her, explaining his morbid desires.

And of their daughters—much to her distaste—Jessica Sue knew all too well. He used to tell her his perverted fantasies as they waited for the school bus in the mornings. Invariably they took place during the Year of Four Emperors, as Vespasian's troops were sacking Rome in the midst of the Saturnalia, and the people who just didn't care anymore, were fucking in the streets. "Slaughter to the right," he told her. "And to the left, harlots and wine." He'd bring himself to a fever pitch. "Don't you see?" he'd scream. "Humanity will not truly be free until there's fucking in the streets!" And yet, his grasp of ancient history aside, she doubted seriously that at the time of his death Bobby could've said who was president of the United States, or—she suspected—that the United States was even governed by such things as presidents. It was as if Bobby lived at right angles to the real world, wandering through it, but in a wholly different direction from all other directions.

The band, however, was a different story. They were loud, yes, and morbid to the very core. In the beginning, they sang songs of the desperado. They sang of gunfire and whiskey. Horses galloped in the scattered drums. Arrows whistled. Standards flashed in the boiling dust. Amidst it all, the Scourge of God hurled himself through his audience.

He heaped vile epithets upon them. Blood flowed. His blood and the blood of his fans. It was a kind of maniacal oblivion, a pure burst of rock and roll release that could never have lasted beyond the nine gigs and thirteen months that it did.

Of late, however, the Horde's music had begun to evolve. And Jessica Sue could not help but take a bit of credit for their new direction. In a summer session astronomy class, she had fallen in love with the theoretical notion of the Nemesis Star, a possible explanation for the periodic regularity of mass extinctions that take place on the Earth. This great clockwork of cosmic death, supposedly a black dwarf, swings round the sun every twenty-six million years, bringing from out of the Oort Cloud a rain of ice and stone. The impact of these comets turns the atmosphere to plasma. Dust blots out the sun for a thousand years. It is an Age of Death.

One evening, down on Grandma Lucy's pier, as they watched the Leonids and shared a joint, she told the Horde all about it. Bobby was beside himself with dread and excitement. He kept pointing into space. "It's out there," he said. "Right out there. Even now the Dark Sun rounds the far corner of its evil path to set its sights on the inner realms of the living."

Later that night he wrote "The Dirge of the Dark Sun." It was nine minutes of epic spacescape, with crashing cascades of electron rock. The tale told of a fleet of Roman triremes commanded by the eight-foot tall Thracian general, Maximin Thrax himself, cruel barbarian emperor of Rome. They were on a voyage of conquest against the dwarves of the Dark Sun, those brainless and mute gods of the outer-realms. Across the moons of time they wander in columns of despair, dragging their beards through the pooled methane lakes and crystalline jungles of that dark void. Tears of sulfur pour from their empty sockets. In their throats rattle the croaking of toads, the flopping of broken wings, and the scutter of rats' feet. But there, streaking out of the sunlit worlds of the inner solar system, flies a great navy of triremes, their sails long washes of kaleidoscopic hydrogen and argon. They trail plasma across a light year in all the hues of the radiant spectrum. With a foot propped on the bow of his great flagship stands Maximin Thrax. Laughing, he shakes whole star systems and galaxies from the wild nebulae of his hair. And with them, falling in spirals of infinite regress, come the marching hoplites, the columns of snowbound elephant, a multitude of legionnaires all assembled in square and wedge. There are horsemen in silver armor, the symbols of their gods emblazoned on their white robes. There are pike men in hedgehog, before a charge. A cannonade. The hiss of gas and panzer troops. The rolling squeal of tank tread. A squadron of Zeros comes diving out of the nebulae, while circling overhead, like a great mirror-ball, there is a lone B-29, almost placid above the waters. And shooting out of it all, spewed out of this heaving galactic sex, out of that coursing plasmatic dark circus of human history and death, rides Bobby. He is bare-chested but for his necklace of cat skulls. He rides a winged Harley-Davidson, his fist high in the air, where he grips the standard of the Golden Horde of Mississippi and screams across the eons of space, "Let there be fucking in the streets!" Thus was "The Dirge of the Dark Sun." Thus was rock and roll. And as far as Jessica Sue was concerned, they just couldn't have picked a better setting for the video.

"Grandma Lucy!" She snatched Bobby's urn. "You're not calling the sheriff. We got us a rock video to shoot. This was Bobby's dream. Don't you understand? He put everything into that song, and all he wanted to do was make this video and put it on Youtube so it'd go viral and get the Horde a record contract. And you know what he told me? He said all he ever wanted to do in life was to show his Grandma Lucy that he wasn't the fool everybody always said he was and that he was capable of something special in life and he wasn't just a nobody."

"He said that?" said Grandma Lucy. She reached for the urn, but checked herself. Jessica Sue towered over her now, young and flush and full of seething.

"That's what he said," Jessica Sue lied.

"Well, it don't matter," said Grandma Lucy. "It's not fitting. This ain't fitting. It's—"

Jessica Sue jerked the phone out of her hand. "Let's have a seat and get on with this thing," she said. "We just need a good take of the band playing. Then we'll film the funeral and that'll be that. Think of it, you'll be able to watch it whenever you want right on the internet."

"He was special to me," said Grandma Lucy, "without ever being on the internet. He used to come over once a month to change the oil in my car." But she had fallen from her role. She sat in one of the pews, with her eyes on the floor, and her skeleton seemed to dissolve when she sat. She was eighty-years-old. She was no longer the matriarch, but just this afterimage of the matriarch. Fallen and usurped. No, thought Jessica Sue. That's not what I meant. That's not what I meant at all. The way she'd imagined it, Grandma Lucy sat tall and proud through the spaced-out Hammond intro to the Dirge, only to close her eyes as the blast of a glass-packed 440 signaled the start of the driving bass. It was to be a kind of ecstatic release of maternal cosmic energy. But even more than the Dirge and the Horde and the video and even Bobby, Jessica Sue hadn't meant for Grandma Lucy to dissolve into eighty years. Already the Horde had gone back to shooting. She and Grandma Lucy were far, far away.

Through it all, Jessica Sue sat with her knees pulled up to her chest. Grandma Lucy watched it unfold, her eyes beady and caged in the powdered rounds of her cheeks. Even the Horde played with a lackluster air, slipping back into the roles of the second-rate bar musicians they were without Bobby. Only Shauna tried to sustain the magic, with wild swinging camera work. Adamant, she stamped her feet when they didn't show enough energy. Finally, disgusted, she shut off the klieg lights and hollered for Reverend Duey to get on with it. Shooting was a bust for that day. And as the lights died and the church returned to the rainbow of stained glass, Jessica Sue was struck with the fact that not a single Minton, beyond herself and Grandma Lucy, had remained in the church to pray with Reverend Duey. Not a single one had even come in. Bobby's own father, her uncle, had not even shown himself in the parking lot. And as Reverend Duey stumbled through the service she wanted to just stop everything and take it all back. It could be the funeral Grandma Lucy had wanted. There could have been vases full of flowers and clean-looking Christian relatives. She herself could've gone to her grandmother's closet and found an old shawl-collared black dress and a necklace of pearls instead this Megadeth T-shirt. They could have had good people standing at the pulpit with good things to say about a good boy. She could've stood up there herself and talked about riding in Bobby's go-cart and catching frogs and crickets and fishing and raising pigs in 4-H. Some of it wouldn't even have been lies. Certainly there would be no need to mention that he'd strapped M-80s to the frogs and used them as suicide bombers in the neighbors' mailboxes.

 She might've talked about Grandma Lucy too. Said what a brave and honorable woman she was for taking them all in like she had. She might've looked out at the congregation as she said it, and maybe her own father would be back and Bobby's too. They'd have sat in the front row on either side of Grandma Lucy instead of wherever they were, probably drunk. And maybe they'd have the nice and shiny well-fed look of nice and shiny well-fed Methodists. Maybe Grandma Lucy would smile some amidst her tears. And maybe she wouldn't have to cry at all, because maybe Bobby wouldn't even be dead, but just shiny and well-fed looking and nice, instead of scrawny and evil and dead-looking and burnt up to dust in that gold and lavender cloisonné urn. That sure as shit rock and roll urn. Where Bobby lay. Probably chunks of him not wanting to burn up and go. But just lying there in the dust, refusing to unfold themselves and go back to nothing. And by the end of it, she had decided that the video was just plain stupid, and the service was even dumber, and none of it was what she'd meant. Not at all.

After the funeral, they drove in silence. Grandma Lucy stared at the urn in her lap, and Jessica Sue stared at the road. When they arrived home, Grandma Lucy marched into the house, the urn clutched to her chest. It was to go on the mantel next to Grandpa. Jessica Sue stood in the yard, appreciating the tall grass, which Bobby would've mowed and the garbage cans which had not been set out to the road. She walked down to the fetid man-made lake on which Grandpa had built the house. She knew she would not find Uncle Frank down there, with his fishing pole and a cooler full of beer. He still had nine months on the original twenty for battery, and his behavior at county had not disposed the sheriff to grant him a furlough. She held her arms around her chest and cried, thinking of him in jail like that, bastard that he was. When they were little, Uncle Frank and Daddy used to disappear for long stretches. Sometimes they'd come home rich, all watch chains and wingtips. They handed out dollars to all the cousins. She remembered sitting on Uncle Frank's knee one Christmas, taking sips of whiskey from a silver flask. And then again sometimes they'd come home broke, and there'd be no whiskey and no silver but just flecks of blood in the commode.

    Once when she was a child, she'd seen Uncle Frank try to kill a man. It was one Sunday, and they were up at this shot shack on Mendenhall—Daddy, Uncle Frank, and Grandpa too. She and Bobby were waiting on them in the cab of Grandpa's truck. They said they'd only be a minute, but probably an hour had gone by. One moment there was the sound of laughter from the shack. Then Uncle Frank and another man came boiling out the door and rolling in the gravel. Men burst from the place, howling and breaking glass. They heard the sound of wrenched and splintered wood. Uncle Frank had his man by the shirt collar, and he dragged him to the front of Grandpa's truck. With his knee he got the man's head down a few feet behind the tire, and he was yelling for Bobby to drop the truck out of gear. Bobby'd crept forward and he put his hand on the stick and Uncle Frank kept yelling for him to just knock it out of gear and Bobby was crying, sobbing with his hand on the stick and he might've done it too, she'd reached out to stop him and he just seemed to explode. He hurled himself away from the shifter, slamming into the window. And then somebody came and dragged Uncle Frank away, and the men went back inside the shack. They all fell to drinking again and she and Bobby held hands in the cab. They said nothing between them at all. Finally, after a couple of hours, Grandma Lucy found them. She must've walked ten miles down Mendenhall from the house.

Jessica Sue called for the dogs and she kicked at the rocks along the path from the house. And she thought about Uncle Frank, who should've been there. "It was a good service," she said, though there was no one to hear, and they would've understood nothing, so broken was her voice in the heaves of tears that rolled out of her. She walked to the pier and collapsed to the boards. One of the collies came up to lick her face and she buried herself in the dog's neck and cried. The reeds near the shoreline reverberated with the overwhelming sound of crickets. It was so hot and buggy. After a while, she wiped the tears from her cheeks, and she went to the garage, where she found the mower and the gas can. She filled the mower and she pushed it to the lawn. She pulled the cord until it turned over. Then, she set the throttle and began to walk in neat rows back and forth across the yard, while a swarm of horseflies bit her on the arms and neck.

That evening she found Grandma Lucy in the kitchen, where she stood over the sink scrubbing the dirt off potatoes. She had been crying and she dropped the potato she was scrubbing.

"I'm sorry for Uncle Frank," said Jessica Sue.

"I don't know what I did wrong," said Grandma Lucy.

"You didn't do anything wrong."

"I must've," she said. "Not a one of these children turned out decent."

"Bobby wasn't so bad," said Jessica Sue. "He was getting better."

"No," said Grandma Lucy. "No. You were right. He was a lot of things, but a good boy was never one of them. Come take a look at this." She dried her hands on a kitchen towel and smoothed her apron. She took a last look around the kitchen to see that it was in order, and they walked to the living room, where she led Jessica Sue to the mantelpiece and the urns. There were two lace doilies now, one for grandpa and his dull-colored pewter urn and the other for the gold and lavender cloisonné explosion of Bobby's. She climbed the step ladder, while Jessica Sue got on her tiptoes. They were at about the same height, breathing the same air, and she could hear the labor in Grandma Lucy's lungs. The Elvis Presley commemorative dishware was dusty. Cobwebs trailed from it to the brick chimney, and Jessica Sue made a mental note to dust it off before she returned to the university. Grandma Lucy took down the picture of Jesus Christ. With her sleeve she wiped it free of dust. She seemed to be studying the picture, her eyes darting across it as if to read. Jessica Sue stood beside her with her hands thrust deep in her pockets. She put the picture back on the wall and ran her fingers across grandpa's war metals. She traced the edge of the embroidered figures of Robert E. Lee and Douglas Macarthur.

"Such great men," said Grandma Lucy. "Such fine and honorable men, engaged in such valiant and noble causes. You should've seen how fine he looked in his uniform. He made corporal by the end of the war. And he would've retired a sergeant if he'd stayed in. Whenever I think of those heathen Japs coming after him, you know it just curdles my blood, you know that? It was God on our side in those days. It was God who sent us men like your grandpa and Douglas Macarthur and it was God's hand at Hiroshima, too. That right there was the power of God."

"Bobby wasn't such a bad boy," said Jessica Sue. "You remember that time you came to get us on Mendenhall? They were down there drinking and Uncle Frank tried to kill a man."

"I remember that," said Grandma Lucy.

"And I remember fishing with Bobby a lot," said Jessica Sue, wracking her brain for anything like a decent story to tell. "I remember this one time I caught a ten-pound bass right out there off of that pier. And you know Bobby he cleaned every bit of that fish for me. He was so excited when I was reeling it in."

"Pick up your grandpa," said Grandma Lucy.

"What?"

"Pick him up," she said. "Don't he feel light to you?"

"Light?" Jessica Sue picked up the pewter urn. She hefted it a few times as if to judge.

"Open it up," said Grandma Lucy. "Just unscrew the cap there."

Jessica Sue unscrewed the urn and looked inside. There was just the dark interior of the vessel. No ash at all. She turned to get a better look in the light from the windows. There at the bottom was a couple of fingers worth of dust. Grandma Lucy climbed down from the stepladder. She walked to the sofa and began picking through her junk mail. Jessica Sue looked at the pewter urn. "Where's the rest of him?"

"I seen Bobby one night," said Grandma Lucy. "It was maybe a week ago. He and Shauna had been fighting, and he was staying out here and I had the sciatica so bad I couldn't sleep. I was up and I was trying to walk soft so as not to wake him. But I seen him in here at the mantle, and he was making himself one of those marijuana cigarettes you two smoke."

"Grandma, I don't—"

"I know you do," she said. "It's not ladylike, but I don't reckon it's all that big a deal. Your grandpa used to do it before the war. A lot of the country boys who come down to Mobile did. But the thing is, Bobby was putting your grandpa into his cigarettes and smoking them ashes. He'd been doing it for years now until your grandpa's all but gone."

"Bobby smoked him?" said Jessica Sue. She peered inside the urn. "Why on earth would he do that? It's— well, I don't know just what it is."

"It's morbid," said Grandma Lucy. "It's filthy. I don't know what could've possessed him. All I wanted was for just a normal funeral. Just one moment of him being normal. That would've been enough for me. But it didn't matter, did it? Even dead and gone he had to be strange."

Jessica Sue rotated the urn so the dust spiraled around the lip. She had an urge to blow in it and send the particles flying in a cloud all around her, all around the room, and out into the world. She wanted to disperse them back into the system. Into the stones and the water. Into the grass and the trees. Into the whole swarm of beetles and snakes and mice and dogs. She looked at her hand gripping the urn, and she wondered about the countless generations bound up in the meat of her own palm. If you sit quiet enough you can hear the flux of your own nervous system, that great collision of billions upon billions of tiny stones. She screwed the top down on the urn, set it back on the doily, walked to the sofa and sat. She curled her legs beneath her. "I never knew Grandpa smoked marijuana," she said.

"It was in Mobile during the depression," said Grandma Lucy. "He waited tables in this restaurant and in those days you had to pay the restaurant for that privilege because how you did it, see, was you sold pints of whiskey at the tables and also that there marijuana. That's where I met him was at that restaurant."

"Did you smoke it?"

"Oh, no," said Grandma Lucy. "No indeed. It's not ladylike."

"I don't guess so," said Jessica Sue, wondering if perhaps brownies were more ladylike. Perhaps being ladylike was something she ought to cultivate once she got back to the university. She'd tell these boys that she would not smoke their weed with them. No. She would take it in the form of a brownie. Something they had baked for her special, which was the mark of a true lady. How they took their weed.

"Well, I did do it once," said Grandma Lucy.

"Tell me about it."

"Oh it ain't nothing to tell," she said. "I snuck it once, when your grandpa wasn't looking. I used to worry about him doing it, but it just gave me a headache. I figured if he got that much enjoyment out of smacking his head against a wall, I ought to let him. Lord knows, he could do worse. But he stopped all that after the war. He took Jesus as his Lord and Savior on Guadalcanal. You know he was fighting them Japs—"

"I know," said Jessica Sue. "But, you just snuck it—"

"—and they were coming into that foxhole," she said. "They just kept on coming. One right after the other and they just wouldn't stop and he found Jesus in that foxhole, and it was Jesus who put that shovelhead in his hand. It was Jesus took him by the hand, and it was Jesus lifted him up out that mud and gore."

She was off and running, and Jessica Sue let her mind drift. She'd heard this story so many times. It was like a children's story that Grandma Lucy had always told them. She'd always known it was just a children's story, with blue skies and puffy clouds twisting into rabbits and butterflies, great sailing ships and adventure. There was Grandpa. He rose up from the mud, covered in muck and stinking like death. He rises up with that busted shovelhead in his hand. He rises up and he's about a thousand miles high. Like Jesus Christ. And he starts walking, stepping from island to island, right up the chain of fire. He's out there casting those atom bombs like so much grass seed. Thank God for Grandpa. Thank God for the atom bomb. Jessica Sue sat quietly and listened. She interjected where she was expected to interject. It was a children's story; Grandma Lucy had always told them. Tomorrow she would pack her things and head back to the university, where she doubted she would be anymore ladylike than before. Though perhaps she would never return here. It was all just a children's story anyway.

After Grandma Lucy went to bed, Jessica Sue sat on the couch. She'd drawn her knees to her chin, and she sat with her arms wrapped around her shins. She hadn't turned on the lights and it was dark in the house. But she could see the mantelpiece from the light of the stars coming in the window. After a while, she stood and began to wander through the house, flipping on lights and then flipping them off. She walked into the bathroom and the kitchen, seeing it all fresh for the very first time. How small everything was. She opened the refrigerator. There was a month-old pot of green beans and a skillet full of corn bread shoved among the tin-foiled left-overs and the curdled milk. "No," she said. "School starts up in a week. You can't come back here."

She wandered down the hall to her old room, which had become storage these last three years. Stacks of Grandma Lucy's magazines were piled on the floor. The closets spilled out with old clothes. Across the hall, she opened the door to Bobby's room. Guitar parts littered the floor. A Marshall stack dominated one wall. The guts of electronics were scattered everywhere, even across the bed. She imagined he must've slept in it, rolling in the transistors and solder. There were posters of Danzig on the wall and Black Sabbath. There was a map of the world that he'd drawn. Very meticulous. But when she studied it she saw that all the countries were different. There was the great nation of Zepplonia, for example, stretched across the north of Europe from Ultima Thule to Siberia. And it was covered with myth. On the southern tip of Africa sat Black Sert with his flaming sword, waiting for the end of time.

Centered where a normal map would've had the state of Mississippi, there was a gold star with the words CAPITAL OF THE UNIVERSE written in precise gothic script. She opened his desk drawer. There was a bag of marijuana in there and a box of rolling papers, which she put into her pocket. She was about to go, but then she caught sight of

Bobby's old four-track recorder. And she sat, pushing the junk out of her way, and she put the headphones on. There was a stack of tapes lying on the floor, and one by one, she pushed them into the machine and listened. She went through them in the best chronological order she could figure. There at the bottom of the stack was "The Dirge of the Dark Sun." But it was a different version. An earlier version. It was something Bobby hadn't meant for anyone to hear, much more raw, acoustic and plaintive.

And when the song ended, she popped it out of the four-track, and she stuck it in her pocket with the rolling papers and the marijuana. On a shelf she found an ancient Walkman cassette player. She walked back to the living room and the mantelpiece. She thought about the meat of her own palms. She thought about the version of the song Bobby hadn't meant for anyone to hear. She thought about the children's story Grandma Lucy used to tell. And she thought about Maximin Thrax. Then, when she was done thinking, she took Bobby's urn from the mantel and found her shoes. She opened the door gently, so as not to wake Grandma Lucy, and she stole her way down to the pier. There was no moon that night and the stars were wild and full of pale fire. Pale, she thought, because light falls off at a rate of one over r squared. This is because it has three degrees of freedom. If we lived in a four-dimensional space, light would fall off at a rate of one over r cubed. And then you would not even be able to see the sun. "This is the interconnection of all things," she said, "even space." By which she meant that all things are not merely interconnected in space, but that they are interconnected with space. Things and space are one and the same.

She set the urn on the railing. Beside it she laid out the bag of marijuana, the rolling papers and the lighter. She unscrewed the top of the urn and set it aside. She reached in and drew out a pinch of dust. There were no chunks as she had expected. Fire had unloosed even Bobby. Even Bobby had unfolded himself back to his basic constituents. Even Bobby was just an intricate weave of tiny stones. She took a rolling paper and put the dust in a line down the middle of it. She took some of the marijuana and she laid this over the dust. Then she folded up the paper in a tight cylinder. She licked the gum and sealed it. And she put it in her mouth unlit and let it rest there. The urn she turned upside down over the lake. Bobby's ashes fell into the water. Then she lit the joint and she leaned against the rail and she smoked, looking at the stars. In the morning she would pack her bag and get back down to Southern. She was crying. Tears streamed down her face, and she felt her heart might burst if she could not go now. If she could only wake up in her own bed tomorrow and in her own apartment down in Hattiesburg. But she needed to get that refrigerator cleaned out and the garbage taken to the road. She'd check on the oil too. See if it needed changing.

And she was listening to the acoustic version of "The Dirge of the Dark Sun," the version nobody was ever meant to hear. She could see him out there, riding his winged motorcycle against the black velvet of deep space. He rode amongst the ice and stone of the Oort cloud. He was out there, looking for the nether realms. Alone and naked, he crawls, feeling his way along a shelf of ice. In his hand he holds a saucer full of pale fire. He crawls slowly, feeling his way in the darkness. Any passing body might knock the ice loose of the sun's hold. Any wandering black dwarf. He is out there on his knees, with a saucer of pale fire, while the winged Harley-Davidson lies bleeding in the rain. The blood and the rain filter down the grooves of the asphalt. All his triremes are gone. Swept away in the rain. All his panzers and hoplites. The B-29 and all his trebuchets. Maximin Thrax is dead. He has faded into memory with all the sideshow of human history. And as the Dark Sun swings past, he neither hears it nor sees it. He can only see the stars. He cannot hear the hydraulics on the semi, nor the clatter of the cat skulls on the pavement. He cannot hear the ice knock against itself. His saucer full of pale fire cannot illuminate the ice that knocks loose. There is Bobby against the black velvet of space. He holds a saucer full of pale fire in his hand, and he kneels, reaching out for the Oort Clouds of other stars.

Satellite Mother

Late for school, I was hoping to catch a ride into town with Wayne, but when I got to the cabin, he'd already left for Missoula and his community service at the Salvation Army. Mona was in the kitchen though, making pancakes for her son Jesse. It was warm in the cabin, with the morning sun slanting through the windows. Mona stood at the Franklin woodstove, frying bacon in a cast iron skillet. A windowpane of sunlight glowed on the weathered barn-board walls above the sofa in the living room. Jesse lay there, curled around a *Tintin* book, his hair full of dirt clods from running in the woods. Mona's got this long, wavy hair, the color of corn, and she braids it into a thick, loose rope that she wears draped over her shoulder. She pushed the bacon around with a fork, and a circle of tiny, silver bells jingled on her ankle as she stepped barefoot across the plank boards of the kitchen. I zipped out of my jacket.

"There's coffee in that pot," she said, "and fresh cream from the cow."

I poured myself a cup of coffee and mixed in the cream. Mona checked on the fire in the firebox. She added the last piece of kindling, and I took a chunk of wood from the pile and cut it into strips with the hatchet. When breakfast was ready, Jesse put his comic book down and plopped beside me at the table. Mona cut his pancakes into cubes and poured him fresh milk from a pitcher. She gave him scrambled eggs and a couple strips of bacon. She gave me bacon too and some eggs and a stack of the pancakes. We had honey that she had heated in a coffee cup on the stove, and there was a mason jar full of homemade butter and more coffee. We ate quietly. It was so good, with the smell of the wood smoke and the eggs. When he had finished eating, Jesse left to go play in the woods. Then it was just me and Mona in the cabin.

We'd been alone together a couple of times, talking and drinking coffee in the mornings, while Jesse played, and Wayne did his community service. We never talked about much, just their cow and the chickens and about winter coming on. It gets pretty cold out here in the Bitterroot Valley, especially for a couple of hippies out of Tallahassee, Florida, like Mona and Wayne. We grew quiet after a while, and she leaned back against the rough boards of the wall. Her hair fell around her face and shoulders. In the middle of the table sat a thick candle, the size of a tree stump. Mona picked at the candle wax. "How old do you think I am?" she said.

I followed her gaze out the window and down the drive toward the highway. Wind pulled in the trees. The cabin groaned beneath it. I wasn't really sure, but I knew Jesse was twelve, so I was like, "Thirty?"

She had begun to cry very softly to herself. Not crying really, but just tearing up. Tears ran down her face. I don't think she wanted me to notice, but I could hear them in her voice. "I'm twenty-eight," she said.

"I would've guessed twenty-six," I said, "if it weren't for Jesse."

"I had Jesse when I was a sophomore in high school," she said. "You're a senior, right? You're going to graduate next year?"

I shrugged. "I hope so," I said. "Pop says I need to put more effort into it."

"I just sometimes feel like I'm still a sophomore," she said. "Like I haven't—I mean what the hell are we even doing out here?"

"You and me?" I said.

"No. Me and Wayne," she said. "Jesse."

"You're living in our cabin," I said, which was I guess a stupid thing to say, and she gave me this quick, savage look, and I figured it was probably time for me to go.

Outside, the sky had turned overcast, with clouds rolling above the peaks to the north. I kicked at the gravel. My pop owns all this land, and we've got a regular house, with electricity and running water. It's a little further up the drive from the cabin, where Pop's in the habit of letting hippies live for free. He meets these back-to-the-land types in the ER. He's a doctor, my pop, and other than us, there's not many folks out here other than a bunch of fundy-Mormons down south around Stevensville. To the west of us are the Bitterroot Mountains and the Lolo National Forest, which stretches all the way into Idaho.

There's loads of deer and elk and bear in these woods, and me and Pop like to hunt them with our Winchester M70. It's one of the older models with Mauser-type action, like Marine Corps snipers used to use. We've fit it with bipods and an ATN day/night riflescope. And we've got a chest-freezer that we run off a windmill. We put up plenty of meat for the winters. And Pop makes his own diesel in a salvaged water heater. He brews his own beer. We've got a root cellar out back, too, with a bunch of fifty-five gallon Civil Defense drums full of rice and wheat and dried pinto beans. The shelves are crammed to the ceiling with canned tomatoes and homemade pickles. Stuff we swap off the Mormon wives for prenatal care. We're hunkered down, me and Pop. So, when the big one comes and the cities burn and the machine breaks down, we'll be ready for it. That what Pop says.

I saw Jesse come tromping through the brush in the woods. He'd been up the draw behind our house, probably looking for scraps left over from Wayne's dope patch. The little fucker had this fat jay bobbing around in his mouth. I motioned him for a hit, and we squatted in the gravel drive and smoked it. He asked if I was going to school, and I told him I didn't think I'd make it. He pinched off the roach and stuck it in his pocket, and he was like, "You got a nine-volt battery?"

"I can find one," I said.

"Then let's go make us some hydrogen," he said.

So we trudged up to the house, where I dug around in the bathroom until I found Pop's electric shaver. I yanked the nine-volt out of that and went into the living room to throw a little music on the turntable. Music to make hydrogen by. Like the Modern Jazz Quartet. Pop sits up in the evenings. He'll listen to a lot of MJQ, with the pieces of a carburetor scattered across the coffee table or maybe his flint-lock all broken down for cleaning. In the kitchen Jesse had filled a mixing bowl full of salt water. He took the dish liquid from beside the sink and squirted it into the bowl. He tossed me a fresh number, and I gave him the nine-volt. On the table lay a brown leather case, containing our pair of Steiner, military-grade binoculars. I flipped the lens caps and leaned over the sink, glassing the cabin. But I couldn't see Mona anywhere. Jesse had stripped the ends off of some copper wire that I think maybe he'd yanked out of our telephone. I lit up another jay and took a couple of drags. Jesse wrapped the wires around the battery terminals. Then he stuck the ends into the soapy saltwater, and bubbles began to form along the wires. The liquid blooped up in the bowl and foamed on the surface. We smoked the jay, listening to those spaced-out vibes. And it got real mellow. Kind of soupy in there. And I sat at the counter, while Jesse, he split those molecules of water into big fat bubbles full of hydrogen and oxygen gas.

I was thinking about Mona. How she sits with her feet tucked beneath her. How fun it would be to get kind of high with her and play a little MJQ. I was running with that. Grooving with Mona in my head there. And then Jesse touched his cherry to one of those bubbles, and it was like an M-80. This bright orange fireball, about the size of a pumpkin, went ballooning up toward the ceiling. It never fails to get me. I know it's coming and then, Bang! I fell off my stool. Jesse lay on the floor, screeching like a shot rabbit. Soap suds and dope and rolling papers floated around the kitchen. I held the back of my head, thinking maybe Jesse was killed, but he popped up, grinning. He's a trooper, Jesse.

"We need us another nine-volt," he said. And he was goddamned right. We scoured the house for batteries. We did it all afternoon. Again and again. We listened to Pop's music. We smoked up Wayne's slag. And we made hydrogen. We threw matches at the bubbles, and they exploded and bloomed like deadly flowers.

Around two o'clock Wayne came back from his community service. They'd got him on a drunk and disorderly, and he'd been working that off at the Salvation Army in Missoula. His job was to stand out back of the place, digging through the stuff folks drop off to donate. He'd sort it into piles of crap he thought they could sell in the store and piles of crap they'd have to haul off to the dump. To cover his time and to earn a little extra bread, sometimes he'd swipe something he could hock at a pawnshop. A clock radio or a CD player. But this time, Wayne came into the kitchen holding a revolver.

I was like, "Where'd you get that pistol, Wayne?"

And he goes, "At the dump."

He laid it on the counter. I picked it up, turning it in my hands. It was a top-break design, with a bird's beak grip, and a four-inch barrel. Pop and I know a thing or two about firearms, and I could tell right away this was a British Webley. Not the Mark VI from World War I, but a Mark I made in the late 1880s. It had Navy marks on the backstrap, and it was in excellent condition. In front of the trigger guard it was stamped with the serial number 87. A collector's piece. I thumbed the lock and eased the barrel apart. The extractor pushed out six casing. No bullets. I put my nose to the cylinder. I could smell the burnt powder. "You fire it at the dump?"

"No," he said, his head buried in the refrigerator. "Why? Is it loaded?"

I showed him the casings in my hand. "It was loaded once," I said. "Not long ago."

"I bet I'll fetch a hundred dollars for it at a pawn shop in Missoula."

"It's a two-thousand dollar pistol," I said.

We looked at the spent casings. Wayne took the pistol. He seemed to contemplate the hunk of steel in his palm, along with the figure I'd mentioned. But then Jesse touched off another blast of hydrogen, and the fireball rose above us like an instant sun. Wayne dropped the pistol. Snatching it up, he feigned to backhand Jesse, but his heart wasn't in it. He just stood there with the gun. He didn't even know how to hold it. He kept it on the tips of his fingers. Then he stuck it in the front of his pants, like some kind of desperado. "Let's keep that two-grand between us boys," he said. "You hear me, Jesse? This is our little secret."

Jesse shrugged. He blew a monster cloud of pot smoke. "Give me that, you little fucker," said Wayne. He plucked the roach out of Jesse's fingers and stalked out of the house. Through the binoculars, I watched him slouching down the drive and smoking our weed. He jerked the pistol a couple of times, dry-firing into the woods. Fucking Wayne.

The next morning I woke up late again and missed the bus. Snow had fallen in the night, and a fine dust of white powder lay across the ground and in the trees. The puddles had frozen in the drive, and ice covered the windshield of Pop's VW Rabbit. He was out there hacking at it with a scrapper. Exhaust poured from the tailpipe. "Hey, Pop," I said. I stood at the bumper, but he didn't respond. He just kept whacking at the glass, getting frost on my face.

"What's the matter?" I said.

He stopped hitting the ice and leaned his elbow on the hood. His breath smoked around his head. He looked into the trees and said, "Can't you just get finished with high school?"

I folded my arms. We have this conversation all the time, and you can pretty much just hit the play button and let it go. He's a doctor, so he's into the whole education-thing, and I can see the logic of his argument. He's like, "I know you're into smoking weed. I like to smoke weed, too. But I've got a job, don't you see? I've got a good education already." About this point, he'll start to pacing back and forth, like he's thinking this up fresh each time. "Listen, son," he'll say, "so long as you have a good education, you'll always have access to plenty of good weed. But without an education—typically speaking—you're gonna have to scramble to get your weed."

It's sage advice from Pop. I always nod and agree with him. And I do agree. He's undoubtedly correct. "So do you need a ride to school?" he said.

I'll catch a ride with Wayne," I said, and slogged off through the trees.

At the cabin twin columns of smoke rose from the pipe hood. Wayne was already gone, but I could see Mona in the kitchen in her flower-print apron and long-johns. She was turning a wooden spoon around the inside of a mixing bowl, and she looked very beautiful, with her hair kind of big and sleepy still from the bed. Watching her, I thought about just going away. I could tell that things were sliding in a strange direction, what with Wayne toting that piece. It was as if the landscape itself was all draining away into some kind of vortex. Getting sucked down. Maybe forever. Or maybe it was all about to come vomiting back up again. All hodge-podge and crazy this time. And kind of eyeball. But Mona saw me. She smiled and waved me inside. She'd made pancakes, and they were just as delicious as they had been the day before.

"It's pretty amazing," she said, after we'd eaten. "Wayne finding that pistol at the dump."

We were sitting around the empty plates. Jesse read his comics, while Mona and I drank coffee. I wiped a little egg from my lip onto my sleeve. "Do you really think it's worth a hundred dollars?" she said.

"A hundred dollars?"

"You told him it was worth a hundred dollars."

Fucking Wayne. I drained my coffee and poured another cup. Jesse asked if I could get him some more milk and I did. I still had the bullet casings in my pocket, and sitting, I set them on the table in a neat little row of brass cylinders. I turned them over so the caps were pointing up. You could see where the firing-pin had hammered into each of them. Mona took one of the casings. She turned it around between her fingers. "Smell the powder there," I said. "It was fired not long ago. Those casings were still in it when he showed it to me, and it's a two-thousand dollar pistol. That's what I told him."

She frowned, watching me, my face. I could see her looking at my eyes, and I thought maybe we were going to talk more about the gun, but she looked away. "What are you doing today?"

"I don't know," I said. "I guess I'm not going to school."

"Would you help me with something?"

She took me over to the sofa, where she pointed at the spaces between the logs in the cabin wall. Thin cracks of daylight showed above and below the logs where the caulk had come loose. I put my hand to the crack, and I could feel a little eddy of cool air blowing in. It wasn't too bad in the fall, but later in the winter, when the wind comes slicing out of Canada, there's no way that little potbelly stove could keep the place warm. I squatted and ran my fingers along the old caulk. Jesse sat beside me. He poked it with his finger until some of the white came away in his hand. "Can we fix it?" she said. I could feel her behind me, warm and very soft, and I could smell her hair, and I thought how nice it was of her to ask for my help.

"Pop's got caulk," I said. "Up at the house."

The day warmed. I took my jacket off and worked in my flannel shirt and jeans. Jesse did all right with the caulking gun, but he got bored and went off to tromp around in the woods. When I saw him later, he'd gotten caulk all over his pants. Mona worked inside, so we didn't talk much during the day, but I kept seeing her through the windows on her knees with the caulking gun, all determined and serious. I'd stop and watch her, but I didn't want to get caught doing it. Really, I just wanted to do a good job for her and keep her warm in the winter. After a while she came out and stood with me on the porch. I stopped what I was doing, and we stared off at the road. She folded her arms across her chest and looked at me, then at the road. Her jaw got hard and her features sharp and sour looking. These little creases formed at the corners of her eyes, and I realized suddenly that she had been two years younger than me when she first had Jesse. How crazy that must've been. I could hear him howling in the woods. I was standing on the ladder, and she took my hand and pulled me down close to her. Her chin dimpled up. "Wayne told me you claimed it was only worth about a hundred dollars," she said.

I could tell she had been crying, and I shook my head. "It's a collector's item," I said. "It's a British military pistol from the 1880s, and it's in pristine condition." She dropped my hand and stomped inside, yelling at Jesse to follow.

Around noon I had finished caulking two of the walls. I had the ladder leaned against the roof, and I was caulking along the base of the soffits. I stopped when she came back to the porch. She had pulled her hair into a knot. "I have to stop," she said. "I've got to give Jesse his lesson. Maybe you ought to take a break." I leaned into the top rung of the ladder and looked into the trees. There were still patches of snow in the shadows, but the rest had all melted away. Mona put her hand above her eyes to shield them from the sun. "I could make you a sandwich," she said, gazing toward the highway. I didn't answer. I looked at the line of caulk I was squeezing into the chink. "Why would a pistol like that be in the dump?" she said.

"I don't guess there's a legitimate reason," I said.

"What do you think I should do?" She said. She bit her lip, and I followed her gaze down the drive to the highway beyond, where I suppose she imaged Wayne leaning across the counter in some pawn shop with that pistol in his hand. I can see the pawn broker do a double-take. "Don't you think I should do something?"

"No," I said. "I don't think you should do anything. What would you do?"

I kept busy filling the grooves between the logs with caulk. Sometimes I'd stop and look into the woods. Giant ponderosa pines grow on our land, and up the side of the mountain, behind our place, there's a lot of stout, little junipers and gnarled Engleman spruce trees, like warty old men. As the valley opens eastward, there's rigid horsetail and clumps of sage. A copse of birch trees grows down by the river. They're all dead and grey for the winter now. I could hear Mona and Jesse inside arguing about the lesson, which I think might've been long division. I had put my caulking gun aside on the top of the ladder, and I sat still and listened to the wind in the trees. The cold felt good, blowing through my shirt. In the sky over the mountain, I followed the high, coursing circles of a hawk.

A few hundred yards up there's this slab of flat basalt that juts out over the valley. Me and Pop used to hike to it in the evenings with our binoculars. We'd get above the lights on the valley floor, and we'd bring a meal of smoked venison and fresh carrots. He always had a bottle of homebrew and some apple cider. Pop loves the stars, and when I was little, he taught me their names and how to find them. He taught me how hot they are, and how big, and he told me which ones might have planets around them. With other fathers and other sons on those planets.

There were always a lot of satellites in the sky, too. They'd streak northward on orbits that carry them over the poles. He'd point one out in all of that blackness, saying, "That one's your mother's satellite, right there." Which is bullshit. It's just the goddamned government up there or the Russians. But I used to believe it, and I'd reach out to touch my mom's satellite, so very far away. A dim jewel drifting across the night sky. We used to sit on that rock, and he'd tell me all about her. She was French.

Apparently when Pop first got out of medical school, he went down into French Guiana in South America, where he lived in a town called Saint-Laurent, working for this aid outfit on the Marowijne River, which forms the border with Surinam, which at that time was in the middle of a civil war. Pop worked with the refugees. But he was also crazy enough to take canoes up the river. He'd head into the jungle in a *korjaal*—a goddamned dug-out canoe—loaded down with medical supplies: antibiotics, vaccines. A regular hero, Pop. He'd get south of the rebels and then cross over into Surinam, where he'd doctor up the tribes out there in the bush. It was high adventure, he says, smoking weed and drinking Parbo. They'd listen to worn-out cassette tapes of Channel One reggae and play Toss-the-Piranha in the boat, just him and his Dutch-maroon river guide.

He says he met my mother down there, on a respite in Kourou, at the *Centre Spatial Guyanais*. That's where the Europeans launch their satellites. Pop says she was a rocket scientist.

I have this picture of them together in front of an Ariane 5 on the launch pad in 1990. In the photo, he's classic Pop in his South American dope-runner clothes: a ratty Hawaiian shirt and cut-off blue jeans. He's pulled his Cincinnati Red's cap down snug over his curly, brown hair, and he's wearing dark aviator shades against the tropical sun. My mother stands beside him, smiling in a black dress. She's got on hose and high heels. Right there in the jungle. And cat's eye sunglasses. She's piled her blonde hair on top of her head. But it's fallen across her face and gotten caught in the wind, where it rolls sideways, like the vapor pouring off the rocket behind them. From the photo it's hard to imagine her out in the jungle. But a month later, there she was, monitoring the flow of nitrous oxide, while Pop sawed through the shinbone of a little boy who had stepped on a landmine. They were down there a little over a year together.

I really have to wonder sometimes just what was he thinking, living in the jungle like that when she was pregnant. The two of them going across the river to pluck shrapnel out of people's guts. He used to get pretty emotional about it up there on the mountain, and he'd drink a little too much of his beer and get to talking about how she died. He said they were across the river in Surinam, near the town of Albina when it happened. I was two months old at the time, and Pop was carrying me in a sling. What the hell? One minute they were talking and laughing, holding hands in the road, and then her chest just exploded. He never even heard the report. But he says it was this sniper in the church tower in town. Some government sniper, he says. Probably aiming for him, right? Shoot all the doctors. Fucking government.

The door opened. Mona stood on the porch. She'd chewed her fingernails down to the quick, and I could see blood crusted around her cuticles. "What if the police come?" she said.

"Then, we'll think of something," I said.

In the afternoon, when Pop came home, I was finishing up at the cabin. I'd worked straight through the day, and I was exhausted. He parked the Rabbit and started toward the house, but when he saw me, he stopped and came down to stand under the ladder. Jesse was tearing around in the woods, and Mona was inside, caulking in the loft. "I see you've found a trade," he said.

"Have you seen this place?"

"I'm a doctor, not a landlord," he said. Which is humor from Pop. "Anyway, you're the one who's in trouble here. The school called. You never showed up today."

"I guess not," I said.

"Look," he said. "I understand. All right? But for Christ sake, I have a profession. Can't you just keep it together long enough to get a job? What do you want in life?"

That made me quiet, and I tried to look contemplative. But the wind just blew right through me on the ladder, because the truth is I didn't want anything at all, but just to fill up those chinks with caulk and then to smoke a little weed with Mona, and I guess maybe to kiss her on the floor of that cabin. "Not a goddamned thing," I said. Which I thought would've finished the subject. But actually I guess he was really worried about me, because he didn't just kick the ladder and stomp off to the house. He stood there, looking into the trees, listening to Jesse haul-ass around and making me uncomfortable. So I decided to change the subject. "You see that pistol of Wayne's?" I said. Pop shook his head. "It's a Webley Mark I," I said. "He found it at the dump. I think he's going to try to hock it after he gets done at The Sally."

"A Webley?" said Pop.

"A Mark I," I said. "Serial number 87."

"That's interesting," said Pop. "Because I read in the paper today where somebody broke into a house in Lolo— this gun collector's house. They stole his guns and then shot him with one of his own pistols."

"You think Wayne did it?"

"I don't know," said Pop. "Do you believe he found it?"

"Either way, I bet he gets himself arrested," I said.

Mona walked past the window. She smiled this sad and joyless smile and offered a limp wave. We both waved back. Pop scratched his head. He checked his watch, and I went back to caulking. After a moment, Pop trudged up the drive toward the house. Jesse was out back in the woods. I looked through the window at Mona in the kitchen. She'd put the apron back on from that morning, and she was scrubbing plates in the sink, then stacked them into the dish drain.

I finished the caulking after that and climbed down from the ladder, folded it, and laid it on the ground beside the porch. Mona came out. She wiped her hands along her apron, and she untied the string and tossed it back through the door to the table. We stood together in the yard admiring my work. I could smell the soap on her hands and the wood smoke from the kitchen. She put her hand on my shoulder and smiled. "It's already warmer in the house," she said.

It was maybe six-thirty when the squad car pulled off the highway. Me and Pop had come down to the cabin. We had some deer steaks we'd fried up with onions in a little red wine, and we were eating on the porch. It was rather chilly. Our breath swirled with the steam from our plates. Mona had made a pot of brown rice and some chapatis. We sipped our homebrews and ate the deer, sopping up the wine with the chapatis and the rice. None of us talked. Dusk had settled in, and we ate by the light of a candle we'd jammed into the hole on a wooden cable-spool. Jesse had finished eating. He sat on the steps with his *Tintin*, but it was getting too dark to read. We heard the car turn off the highway before we saw it. Mona set her fork down. Pop took a sip of his homebrew. We could all tell from the sound of the tires that it wasn't Wayne's Nova.

"Let me do the talking," said Pop. "You take Jesse up to the house."

"I don't want to go," said Jesse.

"We'll get the binoculars," I said. "We'll go look at the satellites up on the mountain."

I don't think Jesse was convinced, but he shoved off the steps and slumped up the driveway. We could hear those tires popping in the gravel as we walked through the woods to the back of the house. We left the lights out and felt our way in the dark. I had a cold feeling in my guts, and in the kitchen I took the binoculars out of their case. I glassed the cops down by the cabin. It was two sheriff's deputies and a squad car. The woods were very dark. They were talking with Pop and Mona.

"They're going to put me into foster care," Jesse whispered.

"What do you mean?" I said.

"Wayne was arrested because of that pistol, wasn't he?"

"Probably," I said. "But that's not your fault."

"They don't put you into foster care because of something that's your fault," he said.

I put the binoculars back, and I went to the closet in the living room, where we keep the Winchester M70. I hefted it in the palm of my hand. A box of cartridges lay opened on the floor, and I grabbed a handful of them and stuffed them into my pockets. I unscrewed the daytime eyepiece on the scope and set it on the top shelf. Then I found the leather case and took out the nighttime eyepiece. I screwed it down onto the scope and put the rifle over my shoulder. Then Jesse and I left through the back door.

From the house we followed the creek into a thick bramble of dead yarrow and candystick among the boulders in the draw. There was no moon, and we stumbled in the thick weeds. Neither of us spoke as we hiked. We stayed along the creek at the bottom of the draw for about a hundred yards. Then we started pulling our way up the mountain, holding onto the clumps of bunch grass. We dragged ourselves over a fallen pine tree and got onto the deer-trail. I'd been up there so much, I could pretty easily feel my way in the dark, but Jesse thrashed around, stumbling and cursing. To the west, the deer-trail winds down into the base of the draw, but we headed east, out toward the valley. Gradually we ascended the mountain, and by the time we came around the face of it, we'd gone up as far as that flat outcropping of basalt. Jesse squatted on the rock. I put the binoculars to my eyes and glassed the cabin. I could see the sheriff's deputies with Pop and Mona, and there were more headlights on the highway. It was some kind of Bronco, I think, and it turned off the road and came up the drive, lights rolling. And it was then that I realized we were in for a long night on the mountain.

I sat cross-legged, laying the Winchester across my knees. It was very cold, and Jesse moved against me. He didn't have on a coat, just his sweater. So I took mine off and wrapped him in it, and he asked to see the binoculars, so I let him look. The cops had left their headlights on, so it was fairly lit up down there in front of the cabin. The Bronco pulled to a stop beside the squad car, and several more officers got out, slashing the trees with their flashlights. When the wind was right, I could hear their radios. "They won't put you into foster care," I said.

"They will if they arrest my mom," he said.

"Why would they?" I said.

"What if they find something in the house?"

"What is there to find?" I said.

Jesse shrugged. "Something Wayne stole from the Salvation Army."

"Maybe so," I said, but I wasn't thinking about the CDs or the clock radios. I was thinking about that gun collector and his pistols. What if they found those? I lay flat on the basalt slab with the Winchester, dropped the bipods, and flipped on the illuminated reticle. It was a three-hundred and fifty yard shot, a shot I could make with that scope if it had been an elk down there. I've made shots like that before. I watched the cop at the squad car, talking into his radio. The headlights were very bright in the nightscope, and I set the rifle butt aside. I looked into the sky over the valley. The land was black below us, the Milky Way rolling above. Jesse was sitting up, looking through the binoculars. I rolled onto my belly with the rifle. I took a cartridge out of my pocket, slid the bolt, and fed it into the chamber. Then I drew a nice bead on this one cop at the squad car. I looked at the reticle. The drop compensator was still set from the last time I'd gone target shooting, and I adjusted it back, on account of the elevation. Jesse was crying. I could feel him convulse next to me. It made the guy dance around in the tube, so I pushed him away on the rock. "Cut it out," I said. I fingered the safety.

Jesse was looking through the binoculars. We could see them

down there, hulking around Mona on the porch with their arms folded. Jesse was trying to talk, but he couldn't get it out. It was just a lot of shaking and stuttering. But I thought he was trying to ask if I was going to shoot them. "Sure, I'm going to shoot them," I said. "Now cut it out. Look at the satellites and quit bugging me."

"What satellites?"

I set the rifle down and rolled onto my back and pointed into the sky. There were a couple of satellites out there, over the valley, and he rolled onto his back too and lay beside me. We watched them cruise overhead, and after a while he stopped crying.

"Fucking government," I said. "They never let off, do they?"

Jesse held onto my arm. He tried to bury his face against my shoulder, and I had to shake him free. "The government?" he said. His nose must've been snotty, because he choked, and I could hear the mucus rattling in his throat.

"Yeah, the government," I said. "NSA. CIA. Look at them down there. But they won't arrest her, Jesse. I promise you that. I can make this shot."

I handed him the binoculars. He watched the shapes moving in the yard for a while. Then he set the binoculars down. I moved to my belly and leveled the rifle. He'd begun to cry again, and the deputy bobbled around in the scope. I tried pushing him away, so I could steady the crosshairs, but he had his arm around my back and he wouldn't let go.

"You got to let go of me," I said.

"No," he said, so I shoved him away. Harder this time, which I didn't mean to do, but I had to keep the deputy in the scope. Also I was breathing heavy. I was shaking and I had to calm myself down. I took a breath. I exhaled. There was no wind at all. The air was cold and very dense, all the way down the mountain and into the valley. The deputy took his hat off. He ran his fingers through his hair. I took another breath and let it go, but my heart was really thumping. I couldn't get him to sit still in the tube. So I did what Pop taught me. I closed my eyes. I fell into the rhythm of my heart and lungs. I breathed normal. I breathed easy. Your muscles need the oxygen, and your heart needs to calm down, I heard Pop say. Your heart needs quiet. You need peace to make this shot. I could hear Jesse crying as I slipped down into the rhythm between the spasms of my heart. I took hold of the jerking muscle in my chest, and I smoothed it out. I let it all go. I breathed deep and when I opened my eyes, my heart was beating at a perfect sixty beats per-minute. The deputy had put his hat back on his head. He was steady in the tube.

"Why'd you shove me?" said Jesse.

"I didn't shove you," I said.

Are you going to shoot them or what?"

"I will if you'll shut up," I said, but the deputy was dancing in the tube again. "Sit over there and be quiet," I said, and I could hear Jesse sniffling, sucking the snot back into his head.

"Will you please be quiet," I hissed.

"I am being quiet," he said.

I scanned laterally with the scope, looking for other targets. Then I saw Mona. Her hair had fallen out of the knot on her head. She spoke with a deputy. Her arms were folded, and I think she wasn't too happy about the conversation. I could see it in her body language. "I bet they've arrested your old man," I said.

"He's not my old man," said Jesse. I rolled away from the rifle and set the butt down on the flat rock so the muzzle was pointed up, over the valley. He looked at me with this blank stare. It was getting pretty cold out there. "I hope they take him to jail," he said.

"He's your step-dad?"

"He's nothing," said Jesse. "I'm tired of him. I just don't want to go to foster care."

"You're not going into foster care."

"That's what Wayne always says will happen," said Jesse. "He says if he's ever arrested, it won't be good for me or Mom either."

"Wayne's a jackass," I said.

Jesse was crying pretty hard, and I didn't know what to do with him. It's not something I'm used to, a goddamned kid crying. "So, do you want me to shoot them or what?" I said.

Jesse didn't say anything, and I guess I didn't expect him to, but I wanted to let him know that I was willing to do it. If he had said he wanted me to, that's what I would've done. But he didn't say anything, and I didn't know what to do to make it all better. So I just reached over and held him, while he cried and cried. I didn't know what else to do. I really think I would've shot them, but I guess I kind of went a little chicken-shit up there in the end. At some point I fingered the safety back on and I folded the bipods. I leaned the rifle against the rock and then Jesse and I sat together, me with my arm around him. The air up on that mountain was very cold on my cheeks and wet. Down in the valley below, I watched as this deputy put Mona into the back of one of the patrol cars.

"You can stay with us," I said. "Until they sort it all out."

"I thought you were going to shoot them," he said. "You're just like fucking Wayne."

Which I wanted to deck him for saying, but all I did was I told him to calm down and I tightened my arm around him, and he seemed to burrow into me, it was so cold up there. One by one the cops crawled back into their squad cars. Pop stood on the porch at the cabin. In the driveway one of the squad cars fired up its rollers, and then all the trees down there were alive with the shadows of dancing blue goblins. I lay back on the rock, and Jesse lay beside me.

You can see the Andromeda galaxy out there in the Bitterroot. Orion's nebula and The Pleiades. On clear nights in the winter the air is so thin it might just be space rushing against your skin. Back when Pop and I used to go up there, I had the idea one time to take a picture of the satellites in the sky. We really got into it for a few months and bought the whole low-light photography kit. We even sealed off the bathroom so we could develop the film. You get this streak across the negative, like someone's scratched it with a fingernail. I used to have a couple dozen of those pictures, before I realized that the French don't have spy satellites over Montana and then I ripped them all to pieces. I held Jesse's hand, and he squeezed my fingers. I took the bullet casings out of my pocket. I dropped them to clatter among the stones.

"My mother made that satellite," I said. I pointed into the sky at a dim speck of light slowly inching across the dome of space. Then Jesse and I took turns watching her through the binoculars until she vanished in the Missoula sky-glow to the north.

In A Valley of Dried Bones

Billy Wade sat sweating in his black trench coat. In the bleachers around him the rest of the hometown football fans wore T-shirts and shorts. They fanned themselves with their programs, moving the rancid air from one section of the stands to another. Over the stadium a haze had settled and in the evening twilight a cloud of bugs swarmed the lights. On the field below, the band was just wrapping up their finale, and the cheerleaders came boiling across the grass with the whole team of the Beckham Raiders close on their heels. And when Billy's cousin Tucky took the field, his helmet raised aloft, the crowd swung to their feet in that praise-Jesus frenzy folks always got around the big linebacker. Watching Tucky pound the shoulder pads of his teammates, Billy gripped the wool watchman's cap he wore to hide the chicken bones tied throughout his greasy blond head. He pulled himself tight, compact against the cheers. His zits ached.

"He kilt Wilbur," screamed Laura, his little sister, her face a knot of flushed rage. "Don't y'all care about that? Kilt him dead. Wasn't a thing wrong with him yesterday."

"I didn't kill your stupid pig," said Billy. Actually Billy *had* killed the pig.

"Hush. The both of you," said their father. "Let me watch this damned game."

A long-haul trucker, Jim Wade came home to Mississippi about one weekend a month or not at all if he could help it. Bored senseless with children, he left the day-to-day parenting to his mother, Billy's grandmother. "I don't know where I went wrong," she said, as she plopped onto the bleachers. "All my children have done run off and left me a house full of miscreants." It wasn't just Jim. The last they'd seen of Tucky's mother was on the back end of a Harley-Davidson, this new man of hers all beer gut and muscle.

"Mother, will you please," said Jim.

"At least you haven't brought some floozy with you this time."

That summer Jim had rolled into town with a new girlfriend in the sleeping compartment of his rig. Tucky claimed she was a lot lizard. Had this gold tooth and a mop of stringy red hair. In the evening she slurred at Billy how much she looked forward to being his new mama. Then her nose started to bleed, and she fell off the ottoman. He'd seen her a couple more times over the summer, but she was gone by now.

"And why is he wearing that stupid hat?" said Laura. "It's only about a million degrees out here. He'll give himself a heatstroke."

"Goddammit," said Billy. "I didn't kill your pig!"

His grandmother slapped him across the face, and a few of the nearby fans turned to frown. But there was scant sympathy at Beckham High for that weird little Billy Wade, regardless of how great a football player his cousin was. Ordinarily such a slap would've drawn a growl from Billy. He'd bare his teeth. Billy's teeth were enough to frighten anybody, coming out of his gums at a bunch of odd angles. His smile looked like the busted-off end of a ham bone. But Billy didn't growl or sneer. He just held his watchman's cap, because he knew if they saw the chicken bones it was all over. He put a hand in the pocket of his trench coat, where he felt the syringes. He laughed his evil-genius laugh. But his daddy hadn't brought the girlfriend this time or the time before. The Goblin Bride. Jim had let him down once again. And a cold rage oozed through Billy's guts.

It made his teeth hurt.

"For Christ's sake," said Jim. He jerked upright and made his way to the end of the bleachers in disgust. Billy followed at a distance, and they walked down the steps to the sidelines, where Jim rested his elbows on the top of the fence. Billy stuck his hands through the chain link. Jim took a silver hipflask from his back pocket and tipped it to his lips. "Them two can drive me bug-fuck crazy," he said. Then grimaced and spat.

"Me too," said Billy.

For a while they stood in silence, leaning on the fence, watching the game, father and son, like a pair of nested Russian dolls. Around them the hometown fans went nuts. That meant the Beckham Raiders were on defense. Tucky was on the field.

At two hundred and thirty-seven pounds and with a 4.49 in the forty, Tucky Wade was the biggest, meanest, fastest football player to ever play for the Raiders, and there hadn't been this much gossip and intrigue in the netherworld of college recruiting since the heady days of Marcus Dupree back in '81. On the internet the subject of Tucky's recruitment lit up the web sites and the chat rooms. His future status was the currency of exchange across the counters of gas stations from Gulfport to Holly Springs. State? Southern? Ole Miss? It was the scuttlebutt around the water coolers of the big law firms up in Jackson. In barbershops and dentist chairs from Vicksburg to Meridian, not a neck was shaved or a plaque scraped without a passing reference to the linebacker. Looking to the attention spans of their flocks, pastors statewide had begun to incorporate the question of Tucky's recruitment into their homilies. In Biloxi the bookies gave odds he'd sign with State. And responding to a reporter's inquiry, even the governor himself—citing the universality of his office—had declined to say where he thought Tucky *ought* to go. "But," said the governor, upon reflection, "if he happens to pick Ole Miss . . ."

Tucky was front page news. An especially erudite sportswriter, working for the *Jackson Clarion-Ledger*, had dubbed him "the Juggernaut," like the incarnation of Vishnu. Many-armed and terrible, Tucky was a monster sent by God to destroy quarterbacks. It was powerful myth for the collective consciousness of the Mississippi football faithful, and it was powerful myth for Billy Wade too, for in the swirling dust of the grunting crush of body beneath body that played and replayed through his head, there was born in Billy the desire not just to see the gouged-out earth beneath the shoulder pads of the stricken, but to hear them whimper beneath his own bulk and to taste their blood on his own lips, and then to rise above them like the sun itself and to drown his brain in the pounding chorus of the circled host all around. This was that last summer. It was just before his ninth-grade year, and it was around the time Jim Wade brought the new girlfriend home. That was when Billy first began to think seriously about the possibilities of mind control.

    Rifling through the Goblin Bride's purse one time, he had found a prescription bottle of Ambien. He knocked a few of the pills into the palm of his hand and studied them, easing them around with his thumb. He'd seen the commercials on TV and he was intrigued by the prospects. He slipped the bottle back into her purse, kept the pills in his hand, and wandered into the living room, where the Juggernaut squatted in front of SportsCenter, eating a T-bone. When Tucky got up to piss, Billy dropped one of the pills into his nighttime glass of sweet tea. Later, in the silent darkness of the night, he'd crept into Tucky's room. He stood over him as he slept, and whispered thoughts into Tucky's ear. "I have you in mind control," he had whispered.

The girl floated up to the fence where Billy and Jim stood watching the game. Her hair was soaked with sweat from the heat, and she walked barefoot in the grass, her panty hose draped over one shoulder. She carried a set of jelly shoes in one hand and an unlit cigarette in the other. She was dressed in the outfit of a Runnerette, those ambassadors of goodwill from South Mississippi State University, down in Biloxi: the Blockade Runners.

She rested her arms on the fence next to Jim's. The buttons on her sailor suit looked about ready to pop. "I sure wish somebody'd come along and light my cigarette," she said.

"Hot, holy damn," said Jim, slipping his flask back into his pocket.

"Daddy," Billy said. He twisted a fist in Jim's shirt. "Daddy."

"Hush up, boy." Jim patted his pants and brought out a lighter. He struck a flame to it and held it, cupped in his palms, for her to draw. Billy began to jump up and down. He pulled at Jim's shirt, gagging on his words. "Quiet," said Jim. "You get on up the bleachers with your grandmother." But Billy only retreated to the fence, ready to duck if the need arose.

The Runnerette had been watching the field, but she swept her gaze back around and planted it square on Jim as she drew the fire into her cigarette. Once it was lit, she kept watching him, taking drags and glancing at the players. When she spoke, she let the smoke curl around her lips. "It's a menthol," she said. "Tastes like candy, don't you think? I just love me a piece of candy."

"Well, hot goddamn," said Jim. "I like me some candy too."

It was about that time, that a man came up behind the Runnerette. Trim, athletic looking. He wore the red face and washed-out sandy blond hair of a man who works out of doors. Billy squinted. He wasn't one of the coaches from down there in Biloxi. Not one Billy recognized from the TV anyway. But he had that same weathered look from those long summer afternoons under the blazing sun. Those summertime two-a-days. He had a gold Rolex on his wrist; his smile glowed in the stadium lights. "Hey, darling," he said. "Who's your friend?"

"Hey, baby," she said. She let one arm fall around him. With her other hand she brought the cigarette up to his face, but he brushed it aside. "This here," she said. "What was your name?"

"Jim Wade."

"This here is Jim Wade," she said. "Jim, I want you to meet my boyfriend, Marvin Petty. He cain't light my cigarette on account of he don't smoke."

"He don't?"

She shook her head. "That's a fact," she said.

"Daddy."

"Quiet."

"No," said Marvin. "I don't smoke." He smiled as he ran his hand down the Runnerette's hair and back, where he took a good-sized chunk of her butt in his hand. "But I sure do like me a football game."

"Is that a fact?" said Jim.

"Daddy." Billy gripped his watchman's cap.

"I said to be quiet. Now you get up them bleachers."

"That's a fact," said Marvin. He gave the Runnerette's butt another squeeze. "I am a certifiable sports fan. And I'll tell you something, Jim. What I'd really like to do one of these days is talk to that locomotive out there playing inside linebacker."

"You a recruiter?"

"No," said Marvin. "Absolutely not. I'm just a sports fan."

"Horseshit," said Billy. He glared at Marvin and the Runnerette. She seemed to only then have taken notice of his presence, his connection to their mark.

"Shut up," said Jim. "How many times I got to tell you to hush?" He made to backhand him one, and Billy shrank away with a snarl. Returning to Marvin, Jim said, "Horseshit. You're a booster or something."

"I just want to talk is all."

"That's illegal," said Billy. "NCAA says y'all ain't allowed to talk to him 'til December. I doubt *you're* ever allowed to talk to him."

"Shut up," said Jim. He crowded Billy back against the fence.

"My name's Leanna Weems," said the Runnerette. She extended her hand. Jim and Billy watched it float there in the space between them.

Neither one would reach out to take it; they just watched it float. Finally, Jim gave it a quick pump.

"Billy," he said. "I won't tell you again. You get up them bleachers with your grandmother, now." But he wasn't looking at Billy as he spoke; he was looking at Marvin Petty, the two of them locked in silent negotiation. "Daddy's got business here."

"All I want to do is bump into him," said Marvin. "See, it's like this: a boy Tucky's size, he's apt to develop him a powerful thirst someday. Might come on him some Sunday afternoon that he wants a co-cola from the store. So, a uncle of his—somebody looking out for his best interests—such a uncle, he might could drive Tucky over to the Quickie Mart. A sports fan like myself is apt to bump into him down there."

"That might could happen," said Jim. He wasn't looking at Marvin anymore. He was watching Leanna French-inhale the menthol.

"There's nothing illegal about the bump," said Marvin. "A boy like Tucky, what he needs most is a fellow he can trust. A family member who's got his best interests at heart."

"A fellow who'll take him to get a co-cola when he needs one," said Jim.

"That's right," said Marvin. "A boy like that has a lot on his brain. He don't need to get his head all boggled up with driving to the Quickie Mart."

"No," said Jim. "He needs somebody can handle them details, don't he?" Squinty-eyed, he wheeled on Billy. Took him by the collar. Billy gripped his watchman's cap. "You get up that bleacher," he said.

Marvin laughed. "Listen. Leanna and me, we're staying at the Motel 6 out by the Waffle House. You get done here, why don't you come over. We'll set around a spell, and maybe have us a co-cola too."

"I just love me some co-cola," said Leanna. She took a motel keycard from the pocket of her sailor suit and held it out, frowning at Billy, gripped aloft in his father's hands. Jim dropped him to the ground.

He reached for the card, and as he took it, Marvin cupped their palms together with the card between. Then his hands fell away. So did Leanna's. They turned to go. Jim held the keycard.

"Room three," she called. Smiling, she winked. Then she caught sight of Billy and frowned again. She started to say something, but Marvin Petty had already pulled her along, and they disappeared into the crowd. Jim stood by the fence, holding the keycard in his hand. He stared at it, like it might bite him. In the stands behind them the fans went ballistic. Tucky was on the field again. Before he joined the huddle, the Juggernaut knelt in a quick prayer. It sent folks into convulsions of religious apoplexy whenever the Juggernaut did stuff like that.

Fact was the Good News had really taken root in the lives of the Wade children. Billy's little sister Laura was strong in the faith. She sang in the choir at First Methodist; she was in just about every club they had at the junior high; she brought home straight As on her report cards; and she won all the ribbons you could win at 4-H. She would've won another at the Mississippi State Fair that fall had Billy not drained all the blood out of little Wilbur, her pig.

The Good News had gotten ahold of Billy too, but not quite in the usual way. It wasn't long after he began to whisper thoughts into Tucky's ear at night that his grandmother came home from volunteering at the animal shelter one day and found Billy and Laura shooting dice and playacting at goblins and fairies. Straight off she signed them up for vacation Bible school at First Methodist, and it was in Bible school that Billy had fallen in with the likes of Ezekiel. And then night upon night throughout that summer, he'd dreamt of that valley of dried bones where in the swirling sand and the blue sky, Billy Wade held aloft a thighbone. "Oh, ye dried bones," he called out. "Hear the word of the Lord."

And the earth shook. And the graves opened up. And they shat forth their bones. Billy stood amongst the tattered, rotting bodies of the dead, and in the darkness they fell together in a fetid orgy of the damned.

He'd crash awake. Spitting and sweaty in his wet sheets. He'd rise from his slumber and venture into the night, wrapping himself in black rags. He began to tie the chicken bones through his hair. Now he was become Goresh, the Goblin Lord. Ruler of Darkness. He'd slither on his belly. Through the yards and along the ditches. He knelt at darkened windows. He looked through the curtains. He saw an old man in a bathroom once, weeping on the commode. He watched a couple fight with their fists in a kitchen. He saw a trailer shift, rhythmic and furious, beneath a love mad as hornets. Standing on an empty bucket he watched their thrusting in the silver leaf-shadow of the moonlight.

One night he slipped through an open window down the road. There he stood above the sleeping body of this neighbor lady. Diabetic, the doctors had lopped her foot off below the knee. And gentle as fog, Billy stroked the stump where the foot used to be. His heart exploding, he'd gripped the box full of syringes that he had stolen from her medicine chest.

"*Dam*nation," said Jim, standing at the fence. "Lord in Heaven above." He stared at the keycard in his hand. Billy stared at it too. Jim slipped the card into his pocket. He took Billy by the arm.

"Come on," he said. "Time for you to go home."

"No," said Billy, jerking his arm free. "I'm coming with you. The Goblin . . ." It was supposed to have been "the girlfriend." That gold tooth. He had copped a few more Ambien from her purse the second time she came. Coupled with the Juggernaut, the Goblin Bride he understood would give birth to a nation of monsters. His father didn't understand about that. He was just an asshole.

"Goblin what?" said Jim. He tensed, but he didn't swing. He looked at Billy, studying him. Then his eyes softened. He lowered his hand, scouring Billy's face for details. Finally he said, "How old are you, anyway? I can't remember."

"Fourteen," said Billy.

Jim nodded. He leaned on the fence and let his eyes drift over the field and the players. "When you're sixteen," he said, "I'll take you. Daddy took me when I was sixteen. We'll head down to Biloxi and get us a whore, just you and me. Now, it ain't going to be one of these here chrome-titty college girls like that one, but—"

"I'm coming with you," said Billy. "Or I'll tell Grandma."

"You think I care what Mama knows?"

"I'll tell her about Tucky," said Billy. "I'll tell her you think you got Tucky's best interest at heart, when you know full well it's Grandma got Tucky's best interest. She says Tucky's going to Ole Miss, just like the governor. Got the governor's picture right there on the mantelpiece. Points to it every day and says, 'Tucky, you gone be a Ole Miss Rebel, just like the governor.' 'Yes, ma'am,' he says. That's what Tucky tells her."

"You little shit," said Jim.

"But I got him," said Billy. "I got him right here." He patted his heart, but in the pocket of his coat, it was the syringes he was gripping. "I got the mind control on him."

"Mind control?" said Jim. He scowled, spit, and looked into the field.

"That's right," said Billy. "Mind control. I'm coming with you, or I'll tell Grandma."

It took Jim about a minute to speak. He'd look into the field and watch the players. He'd get calm. Then he'd look at Billy and tense up. "I'll tell you what, son," he said, finally. He pulled his flask from his back pocket and took a quick shot. "Next year when you turn fifteen I'll take you. We'll go down to Biloxi—just you and me."

"That ain't what I want," said Billy. "You don't understand."

"Well, fuck all," said Jim. "Damned if I can figure you out any better than Mama can." He took a quick pull at the flask, capped it, and shoved it into Billy's chest. "You get up there in them stands and tell your grandmother I'm gone. You say anything about South Mississippi State University or that fellow Petty or that girl and I will flat out punt you through to next Monday. You got me?"

Jim shot Billy a look down the length of his index finger. He turned and strode into the crowd. Billy stood by the fence watching him go. Even when he was out of sight, Billy still watched the place in the surging throng where he had disappeared. His eyes narrowed down to points, as he buried the flask in his coat pocket. Quietly seething, he ran his finger across the cool metal of the chain link. "You will rue the day," he whispered. "You will rue the day you crossed me, Jim Wade. Because Goresh the Goblin Lord knows a thing or two you don't know."

What Goresh the Goblin Lord knew was that after every home game the Beckham Raiders went down to the Waffle House across the street from that Motel 6 out by the interstate. With this in mind, Billy pushed his way through the fans. He headed up the bleachers to where his grandmother and Laura sat screaming their fool heads off along with all the rest of the poor, deluded, jackass mortals of Beckham County.

Late in the fourth quarter, Billy crept away so he wouldn't get stuck riding home with them. They'd done nothing but pester him all through the game, Laura on and on about Wilbur the whole time. Bizarre as it sounded, Billy's grandmother was starting to suspect she might be right. "He took a fancy to him," Laura said. "I've never seen him like a living thing in this world as much as he took to that pig."

Billy *had* liked the pig, and little Wilbur's death gnawed at his conscience. When they'd played at pixies and goblins, Laura had coined herself the Pixie Queen. She trailed moonbeams amongst the clouds, she said. And stars fell from her hair. She dressed in flowing gossamer robes, with silver bracelets on her wrists. And she brought peace and goodwill wherever she flew. She used to hand over little Wilbur and a baby's bottle, saying, "This is our Pixie Child."

Then Goresh would hold the tiny pig to his chest. He could feel it, warm and pulsating against his skin. Gazing straight into his eyes, little Wilbur hammered at the bottle. Formula spilled from the pig's mouth, down Billy's arms, and across Wilbur's belly. The coarse hairs on the back of its neck tickled Billy's arm. And he smiled at it. Maybe it was just the motion of the pig's suckling, but it seemed to Billy that little Wilbur always smiled back. "Pixie Child," he said, feeling the warm pulse of the pig and thinking about his box of syringes and the failure of his whispered words to bring the Juggernaut to heel. Strong medicine. Then he'd think about the Goblin Bride.

But the next time Jim came home the Goblin Bride wasn't with him. Jim claimed he lost her in a game of Montana Red Dog in El Paso, Texas. But whatever the reason, Billy had only a few Ambiens left. He'd sit with them in his palm. He could crush them up, he supposed. Cook them down in a spoon. And he could inject them with the syringes. But would it do the trick? He needed something new. Something startling. Something no one had ever thought of before. He needed something out of the brutal crevasse. And so later that night, once the house was silent, he crept through the stillness to the backyard and Wilbur's cage, where he sat with the pig in the moonlight, stroking its neck. He called out, "Pixie Child." The animal squealed when he stuck it with the needle. Slowly he filled two syringes with its blood.

A long time later, over at the state hospital, when Doc Goldstein would get him to talk about this time in his life, Billy saw himself standing over the drugged body of his cousin. He saw the syringes raised above his head. And he would describe the Lord of Darkness mask his face became. His eyes rolling back. His teeth bared and his neck pulsing. He used to trace his fingers along the curve of Tucky's thigh, looking for the acne-ridden moonscape of Tucky's butt, where the track marks wouldn't show. In the version of the tale he told to Doc Goldstein, he would always let fly with a screeching howl, as he plunged his needles, shooting 20 cc's of pig's blood into the meat of Tucky's ass. See the Juggernaut jerk to life. See its eyes glowing dull yellow in the pain of its subjugation. They'd take to the darkness, the Juggernaut leaping at the end of a chain like a kind of rabid bear. See their loping shamble as they fled across the darkened fields of Beckham County. Searching. They were always searching. On the hunt for the Goblin Bride.

In truth, the first of Billy's nocturnal injections did nothing to heel the rage of the Juggernaut. Tucky awoke no more susceptible to mind control than he was the night before. However, Billy's second effort bore fruit. The next morning Tucky stumbled from the bathroom, pale and trembling. He'd vomited blood all night long. He was dehydrated, twisted in pain. His eyes rolled. Billy sat at the kitchen table. He watched the beast tremble, and then he pounded the Formica tabletop. Calling out, he commanded, "Bring me the Cheerios!"

The first time he'd tried that Tucky whacked him on the back of the head with the box, but this second time around, there wasn't so much as a whimper. Tucky brought the Cheerios, and Billy shook with excitement. He needed more blood. Then a week later his father came home. This was a few days before the first football game of the new season, and Billy had no more Ambien. However, he found that four or five Benadryl crushed up in Jim's whiskey put the old man out cold for the night. Sadly, just like the Juggernaut, the first injection had no effect. More blood. More blood. But in the end there was only so much blood to be found inside of Laura's little Wilbur.

After the game Billy waited down at the field house, squatting in the dust. He took out his father's flask of whiskey and shook it. Maybe it was half-full. After a while Tucky and a couple of the other players came out of the building. They were combing their wet hair and smiling to their fans as they walked toward the parking lot, where a shiny Dodge truck sat perpendicular to the yellow lines, taking up three spaces out of sheer belligerence. Billy jumped from the shadows. Karl Masters, a receiver, let out a yelp, for which the other two gave him no end of grief.

"Karl," said Tucky. "It ain't but my weird little cousin." He punched Karl on the arm, and then Karl punched him back. Hank Simmons, the quarterback, got into it after that, and the three boys fell to punching one another, laughing and wrestling the way boys do.

"Hey, now," said Billy. He had the mind control on Tucky, but these other two needed diplomacy. He held out the flask. "I got you some whiskey," he said. Hank looked up at the mention of whiskey. Tucky let go of Karl's head, and Karl reached for the flask. Billy jerked it back. "But you got to take me with you," he said. Any other freshman trying such a stunt would've gotten a mouth full of busted teeth, but Tucky had a soft spot for his dorky cousin.

"We can't do that," said Tucky. "You need to go on home with Grandma."

"She's gone," said Billy.

Tucky looked disgusted.

"Come on," said Hank. "He can come. Give me that whiskey."

"You better hand it over," said Karl.

"No," said Tucky. "I can't keep an eye on you all night. You get on home with Grandma. You and Laura can play that goblin-pixie game you play."

"I told you they've gone," said Billy. "Anyhow, it's *me* who is going to keep an eye on *you*." These other two buffoons were one thing. He'd take guff from them. At least for the time being. But he wouldn't take any shit from Tucky anymore. Didn't have to. He looked into the Juggernaut's eyes. Was that a wisp of dull yellow smoke curling in those pools of cloudless blue? He narrowed his squint and thought hard.

"Come on," said Karl.

"Fine," said Tucky. "Whatever. You ride in the back though."

Karl snatched the whiskey, and Billy fell in behind them as they walked. A jagged grin slashed across his face, making him look as if he'd gnawed his own lips off in a fit.

At the Waffle House, Tucky crowded Billy into the booth, squashing him flat against the window. A bunch of the team were already huddled around the table, talking their moronic talk. Billy didn't mind being ignored by them. He had other things to think about. Across the street at the Motel 6, he could see Jim's rusted-out Grand Prix. The interstate hummed in the distance. A couple of security lights cast an unsettling orange glow around the parking lot of the motel, and a few scattered door lamps burned along the block of rooms. From beneath a set of stairs came the flicker of a Coke machine. Marvin Petty leaned against the door of a bright yellow Hummer. He had his arms folded, and he seemed to be taking in the night, content with the slight breeze.

Billy listened to the sounds of the Waffle House: a coffeemaker gurgled, meat sizzled on the grill, glass clinked against glass. Human prattle. But soon the restaurant noises faded to silence, and he felt he could hear the night sounds. The world out there in the parking lot. Marvin Petty breathing in the muggy air. The motel sign buzzed. The fluorescent tubes in the Coke machine made clicking noises as they flickered and the ice cracked and fell in the ice machine. There were bugs in the night, thunderous crickets. They raged in the jungle beyond the glow of the security lights. On the interstate he heard the sound of cars and semis rolling over the asphalt. Their engines fired into the blackness. It was a sound that piled up on itself, then rippled out to nothing. I'll have a fast car one day, thought Billy. I'll drive so fast that sound won't ripple out to nothing, because I will be that sound. I will be that gathering together of rubber and asphalt and I will not ripple out to nothing in the distance, because I will be that distance.

He could feel them out there, wheeling in the night sky, a scurry of bat wings. There was room number three. He imagined Jim's laughter.

His belching. He heard Leanna's crashing squeal. In his head he listened to that fast car as it rippled out to nothing. Petty had gone to the Coke machine, but the Hummer was still there. When I am older, Billy thought, I will be like the night breeze. Now I am the rattle of chicken bones in the darkness, but when I am older I will drive me a fast car. I'll race dogs and I'll fuck whores. I'll drink whiskey from a silver hipflask, and I'll tote me a piece, too. A nickel-plated .25, like Daddy says all the pimps tote.

Suddenly the Waffle House congealed all around him. It sucked the wind from his chest and he was blasted into time again. The now. Their voices rang and crashed in his ears. The mud-speak of ogres. Words like the crunching of mealy-boned rodents. He was among the dull-eyed monsters. The Juggernaut's eyes smoked of yellow sulfur.

"Come," said Billy. "We got to go!"

The Juggernaut turned, disinterested. "What?"

"We got to go," said Billy. "The time is now."

He struggled to stand on the booth seat. Tucky reached to pull him down, but Billy slithered over the back of the bench and into the next booth. The people sitting there let out startled yelps as Billy squirmed under their table. When he came up the watchman's cap had slipped from his head, and his chicken bones rattled in his hair. "We got to go," he screamed. Leaning into the table, he knocked several plates of eggs from the arms of a waitress. Billy hissed at her and spat. He slunk to the ground. "Juggernaut," he yelled, untangling himself of the plates. "I command you to follow. The Goblin Bride is there!" He pointed through the window to the motel across the street. Then he tore off running for the door.

Tucky sat dumbfounded for a second. Then he said, "Laura?"

"Goblin Bride?" said Hank Simmons.

"It's this stupid game he and Laura play. I—" Tucky looked at the Motel 6. Billy was outside, having run around to the window. His eyes rolled in his head. He screamed something unintelligible and pointed across the street. "You're talking about Laura?" said Tucky. "In the Motel 6? Jesus Christ."

He jumped up and ran for the door. In the parking lot, Tucky hauled his cousin off the ground, screaming, "What the hell are you talking about?"

"I can't understand your mud-speak," said Billy. He jabbed a finger to the Motel 6. "But there, yonder. The Goblin Bride awaits."

"Laura?" said Tucky. "In there? In that motel? With who? My God, she ain't but twelve years old." He looked at the motel. Then, jerking back to Billy, he dropped him and took off at a dead run. Billy staggered. He whipped his trench coat off and unfurled the black tattered streamers of his Goresh cape. He had the syringes out, gripped in his fists, and he ran, flying, his robes curling all around. A jagged scream poured from his lungs as he sprinted in the wake of the Juggernaut. Out of the corner of his eye, he saw Marvin Petty drop the Coca-Cola he'd purchased at the machine. Then the Juggernaut lowered his shoulder into the motel door. He slammed it with all the force he'd ever thrown into a tackle on the football field, and the door hurled open, ripped from its hinges, screws exploding. Grinding metal and splintered board. Stumbling, the Juggernaut disappeared into the gaping blackness. Billy leapt. He placed a foot square between the Juggernaut's shoulder blades, and fired himself horizontal into the darkness over the bed, where yet a few muffled cries still rang. He fell amid the bodies. Leanna shrieked. Billy let out a ragged howl. He brought his syringes down hard, plungering them into the flesh below. An instant later he was knocked across the room. Light flooded the place.

"My God," said Marvin Petty, standing at the door.

Leanna backed against the head of the bed. She pulled the sheets around her body. Her throat worked, looking for the breath to scream. A naked Jim, slobber flying from his mouth, lumbered to his feet. He swung to face his attacker, the syringes still planted firm, one in each butt cheek. Twisting in the blanket, he stumbled and cursed. Tucky sat on the floor, massaging his shoulder, while Marvin Petty examined the splintered boards and metal where the door used to be. It was a good second or two before the Runnerette found her voice and by then it was really too late for screaming. She wound down like a dying siren. "You little shit," said Jim. He fell off the bed, clutching his throat. Then he pitched forward, gasping for air as he crashed to the ground. The syringes danced in his ass when he hit the floor. Rolling himself over, he snapped off the needles. Billy crawled to him.

The first one to speak was Marvin. He stuck his hand out for Tucky to shake. "Juggernaut," he said. His gleaming smile was radiant in the dull light of the motel room. "Fancy bumping into you here."

Jim struggled to breathe. Billy got up and went to the bathroom. He took a washcloth from the rack and soaked it in cool water. Marvin Petty put his arm around Tucky's shoulder and turned him towards the door. "You ever think any about the Blockade Runners? South Mississippi State University?"

"Best defense in the South Conference," said Tucky.

"Eleven and one last year," said Marvin. "But we got us a big hole to fill at inside linebacker." Billy sat down cross-legged on the floor. He eased his daddy's head into his lap and pressed the cool washcloth against his forehead. Jim glared up at his son. His lips made the movement to say, "You shit," but no sound came out. Marvin Petty motioned with his thumb toward the parking lot. He took a set of keys out of his pocket. "I got this Hummer out front," he said. "You feel like taking it for a spin?"

"Sure," said Tucky. Billy looked at him. All the sulfur had drifted from his eyes. He was just a boy again, bigger than most, but all too human.

"Get your clothes on, Leanna."

"What about him?" she said, pointing at Jim gasping on the floor. She reached to collect her clothes, and still trailing the sheet, she went into the bathroom.

"Listen, kid," said Petty. "I think your old man's gone into anaphylactic shock there. Some kind of allergic reaction. What'd you stick him with?"

"Pig's blood," said Billy.

Petty considered this a moment and said, "Well, I think you better call 911. Can you give us a minute to get out of here? It won't look good if they find me talking to your cousin. I . . . I can make it worth your while." He took a roll of bills from his pocket and peeled a twenty from it. Then, considering the situation, he peeled another and dropped them on the floor.

After they left, Billy sat stroking Jim's hair. He wiped his brow with the cold washcloth. "Leanna," Jim muttered. Billy stroked his forehead. He looked into his father's eyes.

"It's just you and me now, Pop," said Billy, reaching for the phone. "It's just us."

One time, when Billy was a little boy, Jim had taught him to ride a bicycle. In those days they lived about a mile down the road from his grandmother's, off a dirt track lined with rusted singlewide trailers, overgrown with thorny brown vines, dead washing machines, and junk refrigerators. Jim's deluxe vibrating La-Z-Boy took up the bulk of the living room. The trailer smelled of pipe tobacco and rotting dishes from the sink. A television sat in one corner of the room. This was the year Jim had lost his job as a jailhouse deputy with the Sheriff's Department. It was the year Billy's mama left them. She had awoken one Saturday morning to find Jim and Billy in the living room watching SpongeBob off the satellite. She told them she was heading out for a dozen donuts, and it was maybe an hour later when Jim said, "Well, I reckon your mama's gone." Billy didn't speak. The cartoons washed across his eyes. The room filled with pipe smoke. Around noon, Jim said, "You want to learn to ride a bike?"

"Sure," said Billy.

So Jim got a couple of beers from the refrigerator, stuffed them in his pockets, and they headed outside. It was this old rusty threespeed leaned against the trailer. Jim found a wrench and adjusted the seat for Billy's height. With a can of WD-40 he oiled the chain and the sprocket. On the road, Jim pushed him along, telling him what to do, to hold it steady, and to keep moving. He'd let go for a second or two. They were moving pretty fast after a while, and Jim would stop, letting go of the bike. Billy crashed it a few times, bloodying his knees. Jim would run to him, pick him up, and dust him off. Within an hour, Billy was riding the length of the drive from the road down through the trailers to Jim, sitting on the bumper of his Grand Prix. "I'm riding, Dad," he yelled. "I'm really riding." Billy's nose was bloody, the skin all scraped off his knees. His T-shirt was torn through, but he stood up riding as he came tearing down the dirt road, screaming, "I'm riding, Dad. This is really it."

Jim held him out a beer. Billy braked and took it. Jim raised his in a toast and said, "It's just you and me now, son." Tears had washed tracks of clean skin through Jim's dusty face. Billy popped his beer and took a drink. He looked up the line of trailers toward the road and the world beyond.

"It's just us now," he said. "It's just you and me."

Escalation Dominance

When my husband Gordon announced after lunch that he was driving down to the state fair in Albuquerque, he did not think that I would want to go. I am not the sort of woman who attends state fairs. I don't care for the heat and the crowds, all those tattooed, greasy people with their fists full of cotton candy and soda pop. But when we arrived it was only the late afternoon. There were no crowds as we bought our tickets and passed through the games of chance along the midway. Not far from the restrooms, we passed a stage, where a band was unpacking their equipment. Little knots of humanity stood clustered around the loudspeakers. In one intersection the gypsy caravans of the food venders had begun to set up their grills and fryers. In the far distance the rides stood silent and awkward against the sky. It was August and dusty. A fine red dust had diffused across everything.

"Perhaps you'd like to ride the Ferris wheel," said Gordon.

"Then you could see Lily without me present," I said. "Is that what you want?"

"I'm not here to see Lily," he said. "I'm here to see Eliot. I told you, he raised a sheep."

"I only mean that he is with Lily," I said. "Do you want to see them alone?"

"I didn't mean anything by it," he said. "You might like the Ferris wheel. You go up very high and you can look down on everything, like a little toy world."

"And I only thought that you might like to see the little communist you fucked," I said. "And perhaps that you might like to be alone when you do. I certainly didn't mean anything by it."

Gordon closed his eyes. He put his fingers to his temples. "I am here to see Eliot," he said. "And we won't be alone. Lily's husband will be there. Gene. But no, please come. You're more than welcome. It's just that I know you don't like them. And no, I don't blame you for not liking them. But you know full well that I would not be here if it were not for Eliot. I owe him something, don't you think? He's just a boy, after all, and none of this is his fault."

"No, it's not his fault," I said. "So, please, lead on. I want to see the sheep."

At the sheep barn, we dodged a swarm of 4-H kids who came charging into the midway with their fists full of tickets. I don't know much about sheep, but Gordon pointed out to me the short-haired Dahls and the black-faced Suffolks, as we made our way through the maze of pens to where Eliot knelt beside the Navaho-Churro ram he had raised. It was tawny colored and shaggy and it had these four incredible horns that curved around its placid face. Lily had leaned in to snap a photo. Her hair hung down her back in long dreadlocks set with thick glass beads. She had a gold ring in the side of her nose. Gene was all gut in sleeveless denim and work boots. He wore his beard in braided spikes, which he had secured at the ends with tiny pink ribbons. Eliot had dressed for the occasion in a white shirt and khaki pants, as though he had come to argue his sheep's case before a court of law. He held up the blue ribbon he'd won.

Lily is one of these people who dances wherever she goes, and when she saw us, she stowed her camera and bounced over to us. She'd have kissed Gordon, I think, had she not seen me skulking about the chicken wire. Gene grinned. That's what I hate most about Gene. I mean couldn't he sense those alien hands upon his wife? He was uneducated too, a poor man. And he'd done time in prison. Men like him are supposed to flip out over these things. Murder-suicides are built on such ground. But he only reached out to shake my hand, as though we'd made some kind of a deal, which I suppose we had. I've certainly paid a number of vet bills over the last ten years. How many acres was their little farm up to now?

"Hey man, our keyboardist got arrested in Taos last night," said Gene. He pointed with his thumb in the direction of the stage. "Can you sit in with us for the set? Lily says you used to play."

"At MIT I was in this jazz-fusion combo," said Gordon. "But it's been a while."

"Don't sweat it," said Gene. "We're not like the Dead or anything."

Gordon shrugged. "Sure," he said. "Why not?"

Lily looked at me. "It would be great if you could watch Eliot," she said.

"I'm not sure about that," I said.

"You can take him on the Ferris wheel," said Gordon, handing me his tickets.

"It's not that I don't want to," I said, and burrowing my face into Gordon's neck, I whispered, "What if someone from the lab sees us?"

Lily did this little pirouette. She began to dance her way through the pens with Gene lumbering behind, like a bear she'd trained to walk upright. "You'll be fine," he said. "No one from the lab has come down to the fair."

"Your mid-life crisis is really dragging on," I said.

"I just want to have a little fun," he said. "No one from the lab is here and even if they are, so what? You know, I really don't think I'm going to lose my clearance over something that happened ten years ago. And even if I do, so what? They'll move me out of the Green Labs and I'll finish out my career doing non-classified stuff in the Red Labs with you."

"They're going to end the moratorium," I said. This wasn't the time, but I really hate it when he gets fatalistic like that. "The cores are decades old and pitted in ways the computers can't simulate."

"Will you just go ride the Ferris wheel?" he said.

I pushed him away. "Go play your weird jazz," I said, "if that's what you want to do."

"Somehow I don't think it's jazz," he said.

I looked down at Eliot, who kept pushing his glasses up his nose. "So, do you want to ride the Ferris wheel?" I said.

"Can we get some funnel cake?"

"Absolutely not," I said.

"Go get some funnel cake," said Gordon. "This is a fair. At a fair people have what's called a good time. There's sheep. There's funnel cake, and the bands play rock and roll. So why don't we just for once let the global balance of terror take care of itself?"

Gordon is easily the most photogenic of the senior physicists out at Los Alamos. Possessed of what they call a warm personality, he still has a full head of curly, gray hair. He's quite tall and fit. And so it came as no surprise to me that he had an affair. It's just that I had always assumed he would pick someone with her own security clearance to worry about. I had expected him to be more rational in his choices. Naturally, I knew all the sordid details. Who else was going to prep Gordon for the inevitable polygraphs? There had been a number of high profile security breaches out at the lab in those days, and the FBI had decided to beef up the protocols. No more secret documents coming home from the lab. No more sticking your thumb drive into random USB ports. With the polygraphs, he could always put a tack in his shoe to help him over-respond to the control question, but we knew he also needed to make his lies as innocent as possible. We needed them to not be lies. That way his body wouldn't react. That's why I had to know everything, and why we bought the used polygraph machine. I still remember those hours we spent at the kitchen table, Gordon with his shirt open. Electrodes pasted to his chest. The galvanic response sensor clipped to his finger. Of course, I lasered in on the carnal parts because that's what the FBI would want to discuss. Certainly it's what I'd have discussed if I were in the FBI. And so he told me all about the motel rooms and the afternoon rendezvous. One time in the midst of a downpour, she'd jerked him off in the parking lot at the Safeway. Then there was a movie theater once, where he'd hiked her dress around her hip and shoved his face down between her legs.

It got to me, of course. Why had he never done those things with me? We went to the movies. We'd been to Safeway. And there's a kind of competition that set in. "I could've done that," I kept saying. But then there's always something, some moment, and then you realize there are so many things you can never be.

Like the time they went hiking up north of Abiquiu to Plaza Blanca, this crumbling formation of glaring white rock and striated spires. The sun was hot, Gordon told me, and it was bone dry up there and they were hiking along an old arroyo. They hiked through a land of eroded hoodoos, pillars of limestone. They hiked past cholla cactus and clumps of salt cedar. They wandered into narrow gullies, and they wandered beneath the shade of cliffs, and into these deep pockets of rock, carved smooth by the periodic floods. They clambered into cool chambers, and they crawled up shafts of stone. And he said, Lily's perfume had smelled like the earth, and the tiny bells she wore around her ankles had echoed through the caverns.

At the top of the mesa, they spread a blanket, and they unpacked their little feast of olives and hard cheese. They had a half-bottle of Malbec with them and they lay together under the sun. It was hot, I'm sure, and she would've fought that mad hair in the breeze. She had little places all about herself, pockets and tiny bags where she stores her spells and little charms, her oils and essences, aloe vera and Tiger Balm. And he said she took from among her folds a small wooden box in which she kept a baggy full of twisted mushrooms. And did this concern Gordon? Did he consider the ramifications? Lily opened the bag and she ate the mushrooms like popcorn. She uncorked the wine and she gave the baggy to Gordon. The bright beads in her hair were all caught up in the sun. She was this dazzle of glass in the blue light of the sky, and he took the bag and he emptied it into his mouth, and he said the caps were like hard little nipples on the end of his tongue.

These days weapons scientists tend to be very practical physicists. There's little room for the likes of Feynman anymore, but up on that mesa, with Lily straddling his hips, her breasts in his mouth, Gordon said he was looking into her face and also into the sun behind her, and he said there was a fluidity between himself and her and the mesa and the sun. And he said the discreetness of all things suddenly vanished in that instant and he knew that all of creation was a kind of universal flux. Life is a spasm out of nothingness and into nothingness, he said. I had sat hard as stone through these interrogations. I was clinical. I was scientific. I watched the needles on the polygraph. We were here to save his fucking job. We were here to save our lives. But not only our lives, but the lives of our nation as well. Our way of life. We were at war, goddamn it. But as he told me these things I had begun to cry. I cried these incredible tears of sheer misery. It had grown so dark in the kitchen. We'd been at it for hours. I was faced away from him, and so I do not even think that he knew I was there. He was simply talking, pouring his heart into the void. And he said what touched him most up on the mesa was the stark realization of Feynman's One Electron Theory. He said he perceived it in that instant when he was thrusting into her on the blanket, the idea that there was only the one electron shuttling back and forth across all time and space. And he said in that moment he felt the absolute interconnectedness of all things and he knew that he was one with the universe. He said he understood from that moment on that he had wasted his life. He said his purpose and his meaning had all added up to nothing and he didn't even care anymore that we had defeated the Soviet Union. He and I. We did that. It was our life's work together. And then he began to cry, and I had wanted to reach out and touch him at the kitchen table because I did love him very much. But in fact, what I did was punch him instead. I balled up my fist, and I socked him. Right in the face. I punched him as hard as I could, and he tumbled backwards out of the chair. The electrodes popped off his chest. I'd never punched anybody in my life. But it was just so pathetic with him crying like that, and so I punched him. It was a pretty good one, too, because when he got up from the floor his nose was bleeding. "That's what everybody thinks," I said, "when they're high on mushrooms and they're fucking some girl in the New Mexico desert and they're watching the sun go down. Get over it."

Along the midway, where Eliot and I walked among the games, there were stuffed animals to be won, dream catchers and Bart Simpsons. We passed the stage, where Gene had strapped his bass around his shoulders. He slapped at the strings and made adjustments to the tuning keys. Gordon had plugged the keyboard into the system, and Lily kept checking the sound in her microphone. There's a kind of ooze about a crowd, with all those bodies blending together out there. Eliot and I slogged through the mob. We passed the funhouse, where goblins dripped blood from their rotted mouths. We had met before, but this was the first time Eliot and I had ever been alone together.

"Do you have any other children?" he said.

"We never wanted any," I said. "We had our work." In fact, this was all supposed to have ended at the Starbucks when I slid the envelope across the table. It was Gordon who decided that he needed the school plays and the soccer games. I assumed they would tell him to get lost. I figured Gene at the very least would've beaten him up. But no. They were only too accommodating. And then of course it made sense why. They never asked for anything explicitly. They just talked about their dreams. Their needs. The acreage they wanted. The sheep. The spinning wheel. The loom. But I knew what they meant. They'd need a new vaccinator. The truck had a broken axle. Gordon would come home and tell me about it. And then I'd head down to the bank and move the money around.

"You work at the lab," said Eliot. "You build nuclear bombs."

"We've dedicated our lives to protecting people like you," I said. There were lines waiting for the drop-tower and the bumper cars. We squeezed between families huddled together in the crowds. The air smelled of floral perfume and stale beer, and I felt sick to my stomach as I pushed through the bodies.

In the intersection where the food venders had set up their trailers, people gnawed at turkey legs. They stuffed their mouths with cotton candy and caramel apples. There were grills heaped with sausages and onions. Gobs of cheese fell off the slabs of pizzas. We found the line for the funnel cake. I ordered two of them, doused in powdered sugar, and the man dribbled the batter into a long vat full of rancid grease. We found ourselves waiting in a small group, jammed between a man in a tractor cap and a couple of fat sisters with about five toddlers between them. The man kept spitting Skoal juice onto the ground.

"Did you ever do a test shot?" said Eliot.

The man took our funnel cakes from the grease. He set them in a rack to dry, while I dug the money from my pocket. "Did your mom and dad tell you to ask me that?"

"My dad?"

"Gene," I said. I paid for the funnel cakes and handed one to Eliot.

"Gene's not my dad," he said. He ripped off a wad of fried dough. His face was crusted with powdered sugar. "Gordon's my dad. It's just that you're not my mom."

Even now, I cannot say there was an instant of thought. Not a word or even the flash of a word split my mind. It was barely even a feeling, it was so quick, and only later did the dread start to crawl up my throat. My mouth was full of hot funnel cake and I'd burned my tongue. I was angry about that. And there were all the people around me, these barbarians. The sisters. Their little kids crawling all over them like angry spiders. And there was the smell of the man's Skoal spit. You know when you smell something, it's actually a tiny piece of that thing that's gone up your nose. That's what I was smelling. The slobber that had been in that man's mouth. It was now actually touching my brain. But that's no excuse for what happened. There's no excuse for it. And I don't believe that I have ever tried to imply that there was. I felt this ripping in my chest. It was like my heart had suddenly decided to beat itself inside out. I didn't even see it happen. All I saw was the end of it and it was only afterwards that I even became conscious of it. We had been in the world before and then suddenly we were in the world after and Eliot was on his knees reaching for his glasses that had gone skittering across the pavement. His funnel cake hit the ground. He turned to look at me and his eyes were like two moons above the stunned and terrified O of his mouth. I was looking at the palm of my hand, which stung, as though I'd shoved it through a wasps' nest. The sisters went silent. One clapped her face. My open hand. Eliot's red cheek.

    I reached down to grab his arm, but he bolted into the crowd, into the silence. They were all looking at me. They had all turned to stare, it seemed. And they were nudging one another and pointing. The man in the tractor cap spit at the ground. I dropped my funnel cake. I snatched up his glasses, and charged into the midway. For a moment he was lost in the crowd, but then I caught sight of him at the carousel. He dodged under arms and around strollers. I ran opposite, but when I made the far side, there was no Eliot. He'd jumped the barricade. I saw him once, crouched between the horses, the riders. But when it came around again, he was gone. I circled twice, but there were so many people. And I ran back to the funnel cake trailer. And I ran back to the carousel. And I ran down the midway until I couldn't breathe, but there were so many people, their voices a dull roar. I stopped in front of the funhouse, where I braced against my knees. I hung my head, and I guess I must've looked drunk. I was in the thick of them, suddenly. They'd been gathering all afternoon, these people, surging up and down the midway. They were heading for the stage, most of them. Gene's band had begun to play. And they were pouring all around me. I called out his name. I cupped my hands around my mouth and shouted. They were slamming into me, and I was in this jam of bodies, and I kept calling out his name, until after a while, some of the drunks began to call out too. Then I found myself moving with the bodies, this stream of people. They were carrying me forward and when I looked up I saw Lily twirling on the stage. She was this great flutter of calico scarves, and it was such an incredible press of bodies, a mob, and I had to fight my way past them. I struggled through their purses, their arms and their hair. And when I finally got back to the midway, I began to turn in slow circles. I leapt to my toes, but nowhere that I looked did I see Eliot. I turned and turned, and all the while I was lost in the seething oblivion of this vast throng.

There is an instant during the detonation of a nuclear device when the implosion has triggered the primary, but the ablation pressure from the resulting X-rays has not yet compressed the secondary. Using the world's most powerful computers to model this instant and the resulting forces is what Gordon does at the lab. It's a fraction of a second. And yet a trillion trillion possibilities play out across the instant between the trigger and the fireball. I have often wondered what the machine would spit out if some flash of my own life were fed into it and I was crunched down to my basic probabilities. Would I detonate as planned? Or does every instant contain a multitude of worlds?

When I found Eliot, he was sitting cross-legged on the ground near one of the bathrooms. He looked bitter when he saw me. He'd been crying, and his face was dirty and smeared. I squatted on the pavement. The sun was no longer overhead. The air had grown almost cool. I was still shaking with adrenalin and I wanted to say that I was sorry, and that I shouldn't have reacted like that. I shouldn't have reacted at all. Of course, I could see the future that lay stretched before me, a dead land covered in wrecked scabs. And I'd done everything right. I'd stuck with Gordon even after the affair. I taught him to lie on the polygraph. All these years I had waited and waited. Someday they were going to end the moratorium, and I'd kept myself ready all these years. Ready to go back into the Green Labs and the real work and to head out into the desert with Gordon and bury the device deep down in the ground. I was going to be there again when the count ticked down to zero. But then here I'd thrown it all away. All that careful work and planning and control. I'd tossed it all away in a single irredeemable flash of rage. I was no better than these apes around me at the fair.

"We'd better get you back to you parents," I said. "I'll tell them what I did."

"You don't have to," he said.

"Of course I have to."

He looked down the midway, toward the rides. "I want to go on the Ferris wheel."

"Look, I'm really sorry," I said. "But we should just get back to the stage."

"No," said Eliot. "I want to ride of the Ferris wheel." He gathered himself to his feet, and he stood with his hands in his pockets. There was still sugar on his face, and I suppressed the urge to lick my thumb and wipe it away. He smiled and he started walking and he was not heading toward the stage, but further down the midway.

"We have to go back," I said. But he wasn't going to wait, and it was at that moment that I realized I had no choice but to follow. It's such a strange thing to see the world click into place like that. I'd lived my whole life as author and agent. I was on top of things. I had the momentum. I had—there's a principle in nuclear diplomacy called escalation dominance. A nation has escalation dominance when it can defeat its adversary at whatever level of conflict the adversary chooses to engage. For instance, it takes the Chinese two hours to launch their missiles because they use liquid fuel, which would corrode the rockets if they were stored fully fueled. The United States, however, uses solid fuel. And so we can launch our rockets in thirty minutes. The Chinese know this, and thus we have escalation dominance at that level. It's all very rational. And it's kept the world safe for sixty years. That's what I do. I keep the world safe. Or did. I used to. I used to have escalation dominance over the vagaries of life. But now I'd lost it all and I could only react. I'd felt the shift in my bones. It was both subtle and tectonic.

I returned his glasses, and he led me past the bumper cars and toward the Ferris wheel looming in the distance. I could hear children screaming as they plummeted down the drop tower. The crowd had really thickened, and they were bumping against me. It seemed almost a conscious effort on their part to annoy me. I could feel them touching my skin, and when I saw them briefly, on the tangent, I thought they looked eyeless, lipless. They were like walking corpses vomited out from the grave.

"All right fine," I said. "We'll ride the Ferris wheel."

We were high in the air, looking down on the fairgrounds below. We could see the sheep barn and the stage. Gene's band played and I suppose they were really into whatever they were doing. The people looked small and distant, scurrying through the midway. In the sky the light had grown long and very red. The blood red pupil of the sun sat on the horizon. The first planets had come out and everything was very still. There was no breeze up there and the music sounded thin and very far away at the top of the arc. And I wished we could stay up there forever, but each time the wheel took us back into the seething mechanism of the crowd below. I watched Lily place her hand against Gordon's back as she sang. He was pounding at the keyboards. Gene had doubled over, as if in pain. He kept ripping at the strings of his bass. My mouth went dry, and then we plunged down the far side and they were gone.

 I first met Gordon in the wake of the whole Project: Excalibur debacle, Edward Teller's quixotic attempt to develop a space-based, nuclear-bomb pumped, X-ray laser. It was part of SDI, and a pant-load of pseudo-science, and there was going to be a write-up in the *New York Times*. The DOE needed fresh eyes to look over the wreckage, and Gordon and I were brought in on that team. It was our task to examine the opacities that O-Group had claimed they could establish for the radiation channel in the device. It was hard work. It was exciting, and it felt real. And then it was only a few years later that the Wall came down. Gordon and I did that. Not by ourselves, I know. But we were there. We were a part of it, and we both felt so vital and alive in those days.

 But thinking back on it now, I see there were warning signs even then. On weekends, for instance, we used to find ourselves walking through the botanical gardens over in Berkeley. It was among the begonias and the peonies that Gordon once stopped to ask me what I was thinking about, and I said that I was thinking about the opacity of tungsten. Then, when I asked him what he was thinking about, he said he was wondering if it was possible to use heavy water as a fusion fuel. That's what our dates were like, and I can't imagine anything more perfect. But then we'd always end up wandering into the bookstores and the head shops down on Telegraph, gawking at the hippies and the winos. All that pot smoke and faded denim. Everybody coming apart at the seams. And he'd get nostalgic on me and start talking about the Higher Symmetries, his jazz-fusion combo that he'd been a part of back at MIT, where I guess he played the Moog.

 "What were they like?" said Eliot. "The test shots?"

"Back in the old days," I said, "they used to collect the data in a B-29. They'd get right up there near the plumb. It wasn't like that for me, but even in my day it was something really special. It was this big event and there was always a lot of excitement. Gordon used to make me listen to *Dark Side of the Moon* on the drive out from Nellis."

"I'd love to see a test," said Eliot.

"Nowadays we just simulate it with computers," I said.

Eliot nodded. "But we ought to do it for real, don't you think?"

I felt the metal bar against my knees. This weird boy looked up as me as we swung through the circles on the wheel. The world came up before us and then plunged all around as we rode the arc. He was looking directly into my eyes. I brushed a lock of hair from his face. He had his father's curls, and with the tip of my finger I traced the vein running down his forehead. Eliot adjusted his glasses. There was Gordon in the boy's eyes. They were that same shade of hazel, flecked with green. His cheek was still red where I had slapped it. I'm no pacifist, of course. But as a rule weapons scientists tend to believe in the logic of nuclear diplomacy. Mutually Assured Destruction. Game Theory. We believe in reason. We're rationalists. In fact, other than Gordon, Eliot was the only person I had ever hit in my life. "The physics packages are decades old," I said. "The cores are beginning to decay, and we don't know what that process involves. So yes, absolutely. We need a more robust stockpile maintenance regime."

"I'd like to visit the lab sometime," said Eliot.

When Gordon and I moved down to Los Alamos, our team was put in charge of designing the redundancies into the trigger mechanism for the N-88, our newest generation of warhead for the Minuteman missile. It was a very rewarding assignment for me, because to an engineer there's nothing quite like the pleasure of watching the things go wrong that you have always known would go wrong and then watching your redundancies click into place. Over the years, however, I have learned that life is never quite so rational as a thermonuclear device. "That's not possible," I said. "Eliot, I'm sorry. But the lab—the government—can't ever know about—I'm just so sorry. I'm so sorry I hit you."

Back at the stage, we stood packed into the tight crowd, close to one of the speakers. Garish faces peered around us in the twilight. Girls in homemade dresses spun circles in the dusty ground. I saw a shirtless boy in a dog collar, with a bright pink Mohawk down the center of his head. They were covered in zits and downy beards. One kid had a top-knot, like a Samurai. Red bristles exploded from their skulls, as though their brains had been photographed mid-blast. Red faced, they were sweaty, their bodies reeked of the earth and wet ashes. They passed joints. They passed flasks of liquor. They babbled gobbledygook, the slow laughter of the stoned.

    On stage, Gordon saw us and grinned. He kept banging away at the keys, while Gene prowled along the amps, swinging his bass like a weapon. The band had lost focus, I think. They were leaderless, each of them wandering through a different rhythm, a different key. They were in different time signatures. It was absolute madness. The kind of music played in Hell. And above all that cacophony, there was Lily. Apparently it was her job to sustain a single clear note, like some kind a meteor hurtling through the void. Voice and voice only. A voice without reason or word.

    We were caught in this tight cluster of heads, bobbing up and down at the foot of the stage. It sent ice shooting through my heart to be stuck in that flow of bodies. Christ, it was my husband up there, making that godawful racket. I shut my eyes. I turned away. And when I opened them again, I could see the veins of my own retinas reflected in the chaos of the fairground lights, like the fiery skin of a cantaloupe flung out across the sky. Eliot took my hand and whispered into my ear. "Let's go play a game," he said.

    "We have to wait for them to finish," I said. "I need to tell them what happened."

"No," he said. He pulled me by the neck. I felt his breath on my cheek. "I want to go play a game. And you don't have to tell them what happened."

"I can't do that," I said. "I know. I understand what you want. What you're asking for. But I just can't."

I think people perhaps believe that I was hatched out of a pod sometimes. But I wasn't. I could see how much it meant to Eliot to be able to connect more with Gordon and to win my blessing for that. And I kept telling myself that he had Gene. Gene was there for him, but it was so plain as he stood there in his khaki pants and button-down Oxford, pushing those glasses up the bridge of his nose, that he wasn't Gene's child. He was Gordon's son. And then Gordon hit this piercing sonic throb on the keyboards and it sent Gene into this spasm of ecstasy, and I followed that wincing note right down through the bass to my father, to our living room back in 1962 where I was sitting cross-legged in front of the massive wood-grained television, as we watched along with the rest of America while Kennedy told us all about the missiles in Cuba. There was my father. He'd been a cement man in Indianapolis, where he did a thriving trade in backyard pools and patios, until one day he caught the Cold War bug and took his business into fallout shelters. On the night of Kennedy's speech, I remember we'd moved into the shelter in the basement, and that's where my mother and I stayed for the next two weeks. We had canned goods. We had water. We had hunting and camping equipment, and ammunition for the pistol. I was just a little girl, and it was all so much larger than me. So much more incredible. My mother cried every time he left the basement, and she cried again whenever he came back, and then she cried through the next three decades until finally she had a heart attack and died, and I always thought she was crying out of fear, but I think now that she had cried because the world hadn't ended back in 1962, and she was going to have to go on like that and to keep on living with him as he stalked around the basement, cursing and praying for God to just give Kennedy a little more backbone so he'd go ahead and push the button and let the missiles fly. And when we came out of that bunker, all I wanted to do was to leave all that rage and chaos down in that hole and to close the hatch forever over it and to seal it tight within the earth, like a god buried deep underground. Then, up on the surface, I could push my little button and make it all detonate down below. I was looking from Gene to Gordon and then back to Eliot and thinking these things, and it was hitting me that he wasn't Gene's son at all and that he wasn't even Gordon's, because he was mine.

"One game," I said.

We walked in the artificial glow of the fairgrounds, dodging through the traffic in the midway. There were plenty of games to choose from, and we ended up playing several. We threw basketballs at wonky hoops and darts at flaccid balloons. We played Skee Ball and Whack-A-Mole and we shot cockeyed water pistols at the jittery mouths of plywood clowns. In these endeavors we won nothing, and so we were both fairly dejected by the time we got to the claw game, the object of which was to drop a scooper into a pile of trinkets and to nab something, an aluminum money clip or a pewter charm, or a belt buckle in the shape of a marijuana leaf or a Muppet or something. But there was also this shiny Zippo perched atop the pile of gewgaws. It sparkled in the rainbow of neon. I shook my head. "Smoking is a disgusting habit," I said.

"I would never smoke," he said. "But a lighter is a tool. Everyone needs a lighter."

"What would you use it for?"

"I'd light things," he said. "I'd light a campfire, for instance. Or I'd light a candle. It's a tool. It's fire. Fire is the basis of human civilization. It's what separates us from the beasts. With fire we become men. Without fire, we're nothing more than hairless monkeys. We may as well be little grubs, rooting our way through the muck."

"You're too young to have a lighter," I said.

"You and dad can keep it for me," he said. "Until I'm eighteen."

I squatted and took his arms. "His name is Gordon," I said. "He's not your dad."

"But he is," said Eliot.

"You can't ever call him that," I said. "Promise me you won't."

"Why?"

"If the government finds out that Gordon is your father, he'll lose his job," I said.

"Then you could keep it for me," he said.

I touched the joystick, secure in the knowledge that these games were a rip off. We wouldn't win anyway. I took a twenty from my pocket. The resident carny materialized out of nowhere, with this thick wad of bills. Then, one by one, I began to feed the dollars into the machine. We took turns with the joystick. First Eliot positioned the claw above the Zippo. He pushed the button, and we listened as the servos worked in the mechanism. The scooper descended on its chain and closed around the Zippo. But then the lighter dropped loose as it swung back to the chute. A couple of teenage boys came over to watch, real losers, with zonked-out eyes and major acne, that open-mouthed gape of the barely sentient. I put another dollar into the slot, and Eliot moved the claw into position. The gears clicked. It fell, and again we came up short.

"You don't know what you're doing," said one of the boys. "You've got to hook it on all four sides."

"We can see that," I said. "You think we can't see that for ourselves?"

"Well, get out of the way," he said. "And let me do it."

Eliot let go of the joystick. He was going to give over the machine. It was probably some pacifist thing he'd picked up from Lily. "No, we were here first," I said. Eliot studied my face. I gave him another dollar.

He tried again and it was no good, but at least the boys had realized we were in it for the long haul. After a moment, they slouched off down the midway, back to whatever hell had spawned them. Eliot tried again. And then I took a turn, until we'd pumped the rest of that twenty dollars into the game. Then I changed another bill with the carny.

It took I'm guessing fifty bucks, but we finally won that goddamned Zippo.

It was Eliot's turn on the joystick. We'd done this so many times, and after each time he'd look dejected for about a second, but then he bounced on his toes. He was ready again. He had the obsession. The focus. He had the drive. That's what I saw in him at the fair that night. He was analytical about his moves. He studied the problem with fresh eyes each time. He even let himself lose a few just to get a feel for the possibilities of the mechanism. Right before he won, I remember, he'd maneuvered the claw over the junk, he looked up at me and he said, "Is it a machine like this? When you build a bomb?"

"You're thinking about a glovebox," I said. "You hold the plutonium with your hands inside there."

He let the claw crank down into the pile of trinkets. The tines settled against the edges of the lighter and lifted. I waited for it to drop out, fingering the next dollar, but then it swung over to the chute and the lighter dropped down with a heavy thunk. Eliot's eyes grew wide. He reached in and snatched it up. I felt stunned. I've been a witness to miracles, and yet I'd never seen anything like winning that lighter. There was no butane in it, but every time he flicked it sparks shot out of the flint and he kept flicking it over and over. He snapped it shut. Then he opened it and flicked it again. They were only tiny sparks, these little incandescent globules of flying steel.

I opened my hand. He looked skeptical. "But you'll give it back to me?" he said.

"When you're eighteen," I said.

"Did you ever hold any plutonium?" he said.

"Plutonium is very heavy," I said. "Its oxides are pyrophoric. And in some states it glows. It's like the red, hot egg of some future star."

He handed me the lighter, saying, "When are you going to take me to see the lab?"

"I can't get you into the Green Labs," I said, tucking the lighter into my pocket. "But I can show you the Red Labs. We do some pretty cool stuff in there, too."

At the stage, the next band had come on to play. Gordon and Lily were sitting on a couple of over-turned milk crates near the steps. Gene was packing equipment into the van. The faded logo on the side door read, "Ploughshares Wool and Wool Products." I had always taken that logo as a kind of personal affront, a secret acknowledgement of our little arrangement, as though their sheep farm was some kind of catalyst, transforming our money from the dark side into the light. That's how Lily would've put it, I think. The image showed a high mesa above the New Mexico desert, where a flock of Navaho-Churros grazed on the scrub grass, while this fat, little Bacchus played the flute. There were high cirrus clouds above the setting sun, and it was hard to be sure, but I'm pretty certain there were a couple of contrails arcing into the sky in the far horizon.

Gordon let out a long sigh. "I guess you'll want to be going," he said.

"No. Stay for the next band," said Lily. "Dance a little. How are you, Pumpkin?"

"Fine," said Eliot. "We had some funnel cake. We rode the Ferris wheel."

"No problems?" she said, looking from Eliot to me and back again.

"No problems," said Eliot.

She looked at me. "Oh, no," I said. "There were no problems at all."

Gordon stood. He stretched, popping his back. "Are you ready?"

"No, stay," said Lily.

Gene came between them and put his arms around their shoulders.

"You guys should hang out for this next band. These dudes are sick."

"Sure," I said. "We'll stay."

"We'll what?" said Gordon.

"You'll dance with us?" said Lily.

"No," I said. "But Gordon will. I'm talking with Eliot."

There were people everywhere, most of them drunk. Gene led them into the crowd, elbows out to clear a space. He planted his feet and he gave no ground as the people surged forward. Eliot and I sat on the milk crates. The people were screaming. They held their arms in the air. Lily began to twirl and Gene to stomp, like some kind of sasquatch. After a while Gordon joined them. He started with the little shuffle step that I remembered from our wedding. But after a while he let himself get into it, and then they were all dancing together, the three of them, Lily turning in circles. She was so long and fluid, like a willow. Gene moved with the grace of a tree trunk and Gordon kept doing this weird little head bob. But they were all together and they were happy it seemed, laughing and dancing. Lily took Gordon's hand and she twirled round and round. Gene pounded out the rhythm with his feet.

"Can I see it?" said Eliot.

"For a minute," I said. I took out the lighter and put it into his hands. He began to flick it, and I could see the sparks glowing across the surface of his eyes. Like wandering stars, they hurtled through the darkness.

Pleco Fez

In high school Staci and I used to close up shop at the Hardee's around midnight. We'd drive over to the Towne Pump, where Pleco Fez worked the night shift. He was this older guy who'd swap us a pack of smokes and a fifth of Boone's Farm for a sack of dead burgers. Then we'd head downtown in Missoula to the Wilma Building. Go wading in the Clark Fork. Our pants rolled up to our knees. We'd head out to this jumble of stones in the middle of the river. An island of ghostly birch trees, with a secluded eddy of calm water. We'd strip out of our polyester uniforms. I can still see her wading before me with her fingers gliding across the surface of the river, the black water lapping at her waist. Her skin is forever dappled with the silver shadows of those birch trees.

It was the summer after we graduated from Hellgate. We'd grown bored with the river, and one night we decided to climb to the top of a switching signal over the railroad tracks. Drink our Strawberry Hill and wait on the trains. In the dark, we let our fingers roam beneath our polyester clothes. I tugged at her bra, and she pried loose my pants. I had her shirt open, and I was holding her breasts when this Burlington-Northern lit up the slopes. We were leaned back, facing each other, her bare legs draped over mine, and the engineer gave us a blast of that horn, and I spilled the wine, and the bottle shattered in the tracks below. I was kissing her face. Her neck. All the while that locomotive bellowed down the rails. I held her body close. I wound my hands up in her hair.

There was the smell of diesel, and I could feel that locomotive inside me. The boxcars clashed in their couplings. The train kept gathering speed, snaking into the mountains. Then it was over. And Staci lay back like a crab, her breast pointing at the moon.

"Did you see that engineer?" I said. I gave a train whistle.

"That fucking pervert," she said. There was silence in the mountains. Moonlight on the tracks. We were still breathing very heavy for a while, but then we got to laughing about it. She had those sly eyes. That rumpled burst of pixie hair.

We moved into this little basement apartment and things were all right for a while. Until Staci got promoted to shift manager at the Hardee's. There was this test she had to pass, and she started coming home in the evenings loaded down with three-ring binders full of register command-codes. Technical manuals. Customer service flow-charts. I woke up one afternoon and found a schematic of the deep fryer taped to the mirror in our bathroom. At work she got serious. Quizzed me on product hold times. Condiment order. The job meant a lot to her, and I wanted her to get it, but after she wrote me up for serving dead patties, I could see my time with the Hardee's Corporation was on the short side now. That's when Pleco Fez said he could get me a job at the Towne Pump, and we started hanging out together at the Silver Dollar on Railroad Street.

I wasn't twenty-one, but nobody really cared in those days. Not in Montana. We'd head there most nights and shoot a little stick with the college boys. He was a hell of a good pool player, too, Pleco Fez. He'd stalk around the pockets, all cocky and drunk. But when the time came, he'd line up his shots. He'd think about his leave. He never slammed the balls like I did. Half the time he put one in on the break, and then he'd go on to run the table.

We were sitting next to the jukebox with a pitcher of beer this one time, and we got to talking about that engineer. It was in the evening, and the last of the daytime drunks had staggered into the streets. Pleco Fez wore this red velvet blazer and a set of polarized sunglasses. I could see myself doubled in those convex mirrors. Two versions of me. And then two of Staci, when she came floating into the bar. She grabbed me around the waist. She was all smiles and cigarettes, and I could feel her body shivering against mine. We'd been laughing all that evening, playing pool, stumbling around the jukebox, and drinking shots of Canadian Hunter. "Then he gave you a blast of the horn?" said Pleco Fez. He made a sound like a train.

"Pervy bastard loved it," said Staci.

"What about you?" said Pleco Fez. He glanced from Staci to me. It was an open question, I suppose, and it lay before us on the table. There were puddles of whiskey. There was neon warped in the shot glasses. I shrugged. Staci said nothing. She was watching him. Or rather she was watching herself, reflected in his mirrors. Then after a moment, she nodded. She took a shot and slammed the glass back on the table. "Sure," she said. "I liked it."

"You ever think of making a video?"

"Sure," I said.

"No, of course not," said Staci. "Not for free anyway."

"No, not for free," he said. "Not without there's the potential for remuneration."

"I mean any moron can shoot a video and stick it up on the internet," said Staci.

This was around 2000, and folks were starting to turn a nice buck that way, so I can't say it was a bad idea. Even now, I think it was basically a sound decision. "We'd want to do it right," I said.

"High concept," said Pleco Fez. "Good production values."

"A script," said Staci. "I'm not just doing it with no context."

"I can appreciate your sensibilities," he said. "You're talking about costumes, settings. Allegorical significance. That shit costs money."

"How much money?" I said.

He shrugged, lighting up a More 180. He took off his shades, twirling them as he thought. I watched Staci, her eyes electric, like a couple of loose planets orbiting down the hole of my mind. "I wrote a script already," he said. "When I was down in Deer Lodge. It's called 'The Warden's Daughter.' It's a beautiful story, and I think it's going to transform the genre. I'll tell you what. For a thousand dollars, you can fund the whole thing."

"Damn," I said. "Where're we going to come up with a thousand dollars?"

"Don't be a fucking idiot," said Staci. "I'm not really making a porno."

"You're loving those fryers, aren't you?" said Pleco Fez.

"It's a job," she said.

"It's a hard job," he said. "And shit money. I'm talking about an easy job. A fun job. And lots of money."

"I'll think about it," she said. "But don't hold your breath."

It was last call, as happens eventually, and they tossed us out. We poured into the street, staggering arm in arm towards downtown. Pleco Fez leaned into me. We stood under the orange glow of the streetlights. He put his lips next to my ear, and I could taste the booze in his breath. "Do you have a bank account?" he said. Staci had cut free of us. She ran ahead to turn circles in the intersection, howling at the moon.

"We've got a joint account," I said. She ran back to me and she threw herself into my arms, wrapping her legs around my waist. I held her up by the ass, and we made out in the middle of the road. A throng of drunks surged all around us, this incredible mass of humanity puking itself into the night.

A few days later Pleco Fez and I sat on my couch with a package of lye and a bottle of rubbing alcohol. He'd mixed it together in a glass of distilled water along with some stuff he called *thymolphthalein*. Which he said was a pH indicator. He took a drop of this mixture into a fountain pen. Then he wrote his name on a scrap of paper. The letters went on dark blue, but within a few minutes they had faded to nothing as the alcohol evaporated. I went into the kitchen to get our check book, and I dug a couple of Hamm's out of the fridge, along with a package of cheese singles. On the sofa, we popped the beers, toasted, and ate the cheese. "You pick up some baby food at the Safeway," he said.

"But I don't want baby food," I said. "Can't I buy a pack of smokes?"

"What you want," he said, "is fifty dollars. Baby food puts the cashier at ease. Now while you're back in the aisles, you fill out the check for the correct amount using a regular pen. Then at the checkout when she rings you up, you ask if you can write it for fifty dollars over. Only this time, you use the pen with the disappearing ink to fill in the extra amount. Hit twenty stores and you've got a thousand dollars."

Staci slammed through the front door. She kicked her shoes off in the kitchen and cursed at the dishes in the sink. On her way to the bathroom, she threw a customer service manual at the wall. It had been, as usual, a bitch of a day down at the Hardee's. Pleco Fez took this opportunity to exit.

We'd been in a couple of good ones. Real screamers. We'd pull the pots out of the cabinets and slam them around the kitchen. We broke lamps. We kicked holes in the drywall. Half the time, we ended up out on the lawn, our neighbors looking from their windows. This time she grabbed a pickle jar out of the fridge and smashed it on the floor. I did the same with the peanut butter. "You haven't washed the dishes in three days," she hissed. "And I come home to find you drinking beer in the afternoon with Pleco Fez."

Staci stepped in the glass. Then everywhere she went, she made little red prints on the linoleum. I was picking up the shards when I cut my palm. I wrapped a dish rag around my hand and I went to the couch, where I flipped on the TV. In the kitchen, Staci sat on the counter with her foot over the sink, digging the chunk of glass out of her heel with a set of tweezers. There were veins popping in her forehead. A thin curve of blood oozed around the pit of her ankle bone. It rolled down her calf and gathered at the knee. These tiny, red drops fell to the floor in perfect intervals, like a kind of blood clock. I wanted to tell her I was sorry and I wanted to go lick that blood off her leg. "But I'm planning our future here," I said. "Look at yourself. You're hating every minute of that job. You put in fifteen hour days and you're covered in rancid grease."

She threw the tweezers at me.

There was a summer storm in the mountains and a thick boil of thunderheads lay over the valley on that Tuesday afternoon when I finally said, fuck it. Now or never. I stood in the bright and shiny Safeway, gazing at the happy light glowing off the Doritos bags and the candies. All the reds and blues of the packaging schemes seem to throb with the muzak. I took a basket. I headed into the aisles. I wandered past the towers of stacked chili cans and the jars of spaghetti sauce. I strolled right up to the baby food, where I grabbed jars of mashed peas. Jars of carrots and pears. I packed it all into my basket, adding the prices in my head. Then I wrote out the check.

At the register, I smiled my good-daddy smile. She told me the price. And it was just like I had calculated. I flipped open my checkbook. I leaned into the counter. And glancing up, I flashed my smile, asking, "Please, can I make it for fifty dollars over?"

She looked at the customer service counter. Her boss was down there ringing up a stack of lotto tickets. She looked at the baby food. I don't guess it was strictly policy to take checks for over the amount. The world was changing just then, and I don't suppose you could even do this scam today, but at the time it was still possible. People still wrote checks at the Safeway. Such checks still took a few days to clear. "There's a pawn shop on Higgins has this crib for sale," I said. She looked back at her boss, then to me. And smiling, she cashed me out for two twenties and a ten. I grabbed my sack. I stuffed the bills into my pocket.

In the parking lot, I stood watching the storm roll over in the valley. The street was empty of traffic. Humanity. It was another world. Another plane of reality. I hit twenty stores over the next three days. I hit Safeways and Albertsons. I hit convenience stores. I hit the Sears. Each time it went just like clockwork. Then I took the money to Staci down at the Hardee's.

I found her sitting at the picnic tables beside the dumpster, with a pile of cigarette butts beside her. She had been crying, and her eyes were puffy and red, set in black pits of despair. I made her close them. Then I slipped the bills into her hand, all folded and paper-clipped together. When she looked up her whole face lit with joy. She was breathless. She stood against me and I could feel her heart pounding beneath her clothes. I could see myself reflected in the gold plastic of the brand-new assistant manager's name tag over her breast. In her hand she held a library book on management strategies for the restaurant industry. "I've been saving it," I said. "I was going to buy a ring with it, but we'll get a bigger ring now. This is our future. Just quit this shit and let's get out of here. It'll be just like up on the switching signal."

She nodded. Slowly at first and then with vigor. "All right," she said. "All-fucking-right."

Then we kissed, and she crushed herself against my chest. And when she came home that night, she dumped her manuals and industry newsletters into the trash. We made love on the sofa, like we used to do, long into the night with Jane's Addiction blasting on the stereo. We stayed awake for the sunrise, sitting on the lawn in front of our building, wrapped together in a blanket. We smoked cigs and talked about the video, and she kept looking at me sideways, her face aglow in the pink light that bled across the morning blue.

"But where did you save it?" she said.

I pulled her tight against me under the blanket. "I buried it in a mason jar on that island in the river where we used to go skinny dipping," I said.

'The Warden's Daughter' was this homemade porno book that Pleco Fez had written when he was on Fish Row for kiting checks. He said it was something he could swap the other convicts for smokes and weed. To do the shots we moved our stuff out of the bedroom in our apartment, which was made of concrete blocks already. We ripped out the carpet, right down to the cement under-floor, and we got an army cot from the Salvation Army, until eventually we had a complete prison cell in there. It had a commode and everything, a little shelf for all of my prison library books and a nice arrangement of jailhouse graffiti on the walls. We even had fake bars made from PVC pipe, which we then painted black to match the establishment shots we took at the Old Montana State prison down in Deer Lodge. All told, it took us three days to shoot the video. I thought I was going to be nervous at first, but it was just me and Staci and Pleco Fez.

I no longer have that xeroxed copy of 'The Warden's Daughter.' And I don't have a copy of the video we shot either. But I'll never forget the clink of her father's keys, or the way she squeezed through the ductwork in the walls, or how she slipped into my cell to fondle me in the moonlight. The way she gripped the bars, with her arms stretched wide like Jesus Christ. The way I slid down her body as the shot went to fog in the land of dreams. I can still hear her feet in the clover as we ran through the meadow, where we stretched the blanket and where we did it under the hot sun. The squall of the woods. The cackle of birds. The humming drone of the bees. We did it backwards and we did it missionary, and we did it standing against trees. We did it cowgirl and we did it backwards cowgirl and we did it 69. Once with her on top. And once with me on top. And all the while, there was Pleco Fez, circling through the trees with that Cyclopes eye.

It was four days later that the sheriff's deputy came knocking at the door. I never even got to see the final cut.

ʘ

When I got out of Deer Lodge, my mother told me I could sleep in the basement, but she wasn't driving down to get me. So with nobody else to call, I got in touch with Pleco Fez, who drove up in a brand-new Le Baron. I was standing in the parking lot, looking east into the snow-capped peaks of the Deer Lodge National Forest. The last gate had slammed shut, and it was morning. The sky was a deep, pregnant grey, shot through with the sunlight. The land down in the gulch looked very dry and brown all the way to Deer Lodge Mountain. One of the guards had given me a fresh pack of smokes, and I squatted on the dusty pavement, looking at the sunlight in the rags of snow. Fifteen months is a very long time for a kid like me to be in jail.

Freshly tanned, Pleco Fez was dressed in a peach-colored silk shirt and white pants, and he had a set of lizard skin shoes on his feet. He was like an advertisement for a better life than the one you're living now. It was cold in the grey morning. But he must've carried his own heat within him. It was as though his heart had been replaced with a private sunshine all his own. Gleaming like a god, he snapped a business card into my palm. It was silky smooth, with hot pink lettering, and it read: PlecoFez.com. "We're for the connoisseur," he said. "Totally high end."

We drove north through the mountains. I rolled the window down to feel the free world blow against my skin. The blue sky stretched forever beyond the snow white meadows in the evergreens, and spaced-out jazz rolled through the car. He had a box of Chardonnay wine chilling in a cooler full of ice that he had jammed between the seats, and there was a bag of crackers and a block of goat cheese on a wooden tray. He drove with his thighs, making these little goat cheese set-ups and pouring fresh wine into plastic glasses, and he had a big three-ring binder full of his work, which he laid across my lap so I could flip through the pages. They'd made a video about a dentist and another about a librarian. He seemed to have a thing for the happenstance of occupation. He had a series of Westerns that they had shot up at Garnet ghost town. And there were a couple more prison pictures too. Flipping the pages, I came to this shot of Staci in a pair of cut-off ring-arounds. Some rangy hack with a mullet and a thick baton held her by the arm. They were in the shower room together, and so I guess they were getting ready to take a shower. It gave me this cold feeling to see. Like a lump of wet metal moving back and forth in my guts. Because I could hear the water and I could feel the silence, and they were all leaving the shower room, all the others but me and I could hear this thin trickle of laughter and those wet footfalls coming up behind. I shut the binder. I built myself a fresh set-up with the crackers and the goat cheese.

"I feel terrible about it," he said. "But you know they'd have given me five years."

"It wouldn't have reduced my sentence," I said. "If I'd mentioned you."

"But I want you to know how bad I feel," he said. "I really want to make it up to you."

"I'd like to do another video," I said. "Get paid, maybe."

He looked squinty, gazing into the trees. "Don't get me wrong," he said. "That was magic what you guys did. But we've got a couple of professionals now. Guys with—How do I put it? Look, your acting was top-notch. You can really feel the intensity."

"It's just that's what I've been hanging on," I said. "Thinking maybe I had a future in it."

"I don't know," he said. "It's the girls who make the money. But maybe there's something. We'll see." He patted me on the shoulder. Encouraged me to drink up. Have another glass.

I opened the binder. I flipped through the stills from her movies. They were real professionals, all right. Some really big guys. We didn't talk a lot after that. I just looked through the binder until we drove past East Missoula and into the valley.

He let me out at my mother's place, but I didn't go in. Instead, I wandered downtown and waded into the Clark Fork, where I headed out to that rocky island in the birch trees. Someone had built a little fire scar out there, in the middle of a circle of river stones. They had jabbed a screwdriver between the rocks, and it was blackened with soot. There was an abandoned lean-to, a ratty blue tarp, and a vinyl couch, something stolen from a doctor's office. It had that industrial look. That's where I lay down, and I slept for a long while, until the cold drove me awake, and I was very thirsty. I crawled to the river, and on my hands and knees, I drank right out of the Clark Fork. Thinking, fuck it. Go ahead and kill me. Then I waded back across to the streets, where I wandered aimless for hours. In fact I took to wandering. I walked all over. I walked for hours at a time, all day, just wandering.

They'd slapped Missoula clean in my absence. There was a fresh coat of paint over everything. Even the people looked healthier. More perfect, in their hiking shorts and tank tops. They walked dogs. They tossed Frisbees. It was like the whole goddamned town had been replaced with a Hollywood version of itself. Brighter and sexier this time. With plastic tits.

I got a job at the Jiffy Lube. And when I wasn't working, I liked to head down Railroad Street to the Silver Dollar, where I'd crawl up to the bar and pour quarters into the keno machines. There was always somebody there I knew. Usually it was these two local kids from my days at the Hardee's. They'd been juniors in high school, but now they were clean cut college boys. They had Greek letters on their shirts and spiky hair. They bought me beer, and I told them lies about Deer Lodge. "I saw this dude get shanked at breakfast," I told them. I could not have told them the truth. For they would have left me sitting in my own blood and shit if I'd told them the truth. The truth wasn't what they wanted. What they wanted was to clap me on the back and to order me another round. And I hated them for it. I had always hated them. But now my hatred for them grew and grew. And I hated them just a little bit more every time that I saw them.

 This was around the middle of February. It was snowing outside, and me and those college boys were shooting stick in the Silver Dollar. I looked up at the razor edge of wind as the door opened. It was Staci and Pleco Fez. They were out on a bender and having a pretty good time of it. She looked fuller. She had color. And for a moment I saw her on that switching signal again; I could feel her body through the polyester. I heard her laughter in the birch trees. But when she saw me, she looked gone. She looked dead as drowning. I walked over to them at the keno machines. "Hey Staci," I said. "Long time."

 "Wes," she said. "How long you been out of jail?"

 "About a month."

"You have fun?" she said.

I dropped a quarter into a keno machine and watched the numbers flash. Pleco Fez put his arms around us, pulling us close. "What do you say we put Wes in the epic?"

She rolled her eyes. I came up short on the keno machine, and it gave me that sad little plaintive note. "You're the director," she said.

I fed the machine a fresh quarter. Got the same dead note. "When do we shoot?"

"About a month," he said. "But it's just a minor role, so don't quit your day job."

Wandering the streets, I took to punching people out in my mind. I'd go crazy-face. I'd clock them. I'd kick their guts out. All behind my eyes. I was right there on Main Street this one time, and I could hear them talking. I could feel their eyes crawling around on my skin. I could feel them inside me. They were like bugs skittering through my veins. And then I was suddenly made out of bugs. Bugs and vertigo. And it was like I was about to crash into the pavement. And go scuttling down the sewers. So I started going bat-shit. I started screaming in their faces. I even yelled at this little kid. He had a go-cup full of hot chocolate and he dropped it in the snow when I yelled. And it spattered out brown. And I was like, "Pick it up! Pick up the fucking cup!" And he started to cry, that damned little kid. And I was crying for him too, you know? And he was grabbing for his mother, this kid, and I just kept screaming, "Pick up the fucking cup. Just put it all back together, you little shit." And then out of nowhere some guy rounds off and decked me one.

I staggered into a parking meter. I tripped. And he got in front of the lady, her kid. This Tarzan-guy. She picked up the boy and she held him, his face pressed into her neck. He was crying like you wouldn't believe. And I was too. But this guy, he didn't give a shit that I was sad about any of this. He just took up a boxer's stance, his fists raised. And I could see that he knew what he was doing, and that he was about to really let me have it. Which is what I deserved. And he had a nice crowd gathered around to watch him kick my ass, too, and I wished I was one of them. I would've loved to have seen it, you know? I'd have kicked my own ass if they'd have given me the chance. But it was just me out there. Sliding down the drain. It was just me at the center of that vortex, twisting across the pavement with all that soapy water. All that blood and shit, and those skittering bugs in my mind.

    I turned and ran, and I cut up a side street, but no one followed me. And after a while I slowed down to a walk again. Eventually, I found a liquor store and got a pint of gin. I was out on the streets, and the sky had turned overcast and grey. I pulled my coat against the sleet, and I dodged through the crowds, making my way down to the river. There I sat on a park bench, watching the rain drizzle in the choppy water. I drank the gin. And then somewhere in there I must have decided to stagger out to that island in the Clark Fork. The cold water burned into my feet and legs. I stumbled once and went under. And when I came up, I was dripping wet and gasping. The water steamed off my clothes and hair. I dragged myself onto the stones, where I could barely breathe. But I knew I had to get dry. I rolled to my feet. At the campsite, I found a stern-o can with a little left, which I lit. And I wrapped myself in the blue tarp. I looked around for any small twigs that I might dry and ignite. It was meager pickings, with nothing to start it with, other than a soggy heap of toilet paper buried in the thin snow. The blackened screwdriver still lay among the stones. Convulsing with cold, I squatted by the wet ash. I took the screwdriver in my hands. I sat cross-legged. I listened to the wind. I lost my gin in the river.

    Eventually I stood, tucking the screwdriver into my back pocket. It was late afternoon, and the grey sky hung close to the earth. Snow had begun to fall in thick, wet flakes that melted on my skin.

Pleco Fez had a warehouse now, where he shot the videos. It was quite the production. He had a guy holding a boom mic. He had two different cameramen. He had a couple of computers and a bunch of klieg lights. There was a sound panel and a director's chair. He had a light meter, and he kept wandering around taking readings off the actors' butts, their tits. Then he'd call some flunky over to powder up a bright spot. They'd built a nice set with tall columns and porticos. The walls were painted with a profusion of grapes and cherubs. Goat-boys and mermaids. They had a stuffed pig with an apple in its mouth. They had crowing roosters walking all over the place. They had a boa constrictor. They had a case of Reddi-wip and a ten pound bag of strawberries.

But when the time came, I couldn't do it. I wasn't even in the main shot. I was just part of the background orgy. So nobody was really interested in being patient with me. The guys from the three-ring binder were on the set. The professionals, with their giant cocks. They stood around flexing their butts and working on their erections. A couple of the girls had come out to help them, though not Staci. That wasn't her job. I stood watching them for a while. Then this girl came up to me and it was my turn. She took a hold of my penis and pumped it back and forth. All pretty mechanical. She was chewing her gum. And she had crooked teeth, I remember, but they were not badly crooked. And I think she might've been a nice girl. She smiled at me while she did it. Which is friendly enough. But it was the kind of smile you'd get down at the DMV.

"Hurry up," she whispered. "They're getting ready to start."

Staci had come out of the back room. She dropped her robe on the concrete and took up her position in this swing set hung between the columns. One of the roosters pecked at my foot. I was watching one of the professionals get a blowjob. The guy with the mullet. He could flex his pecs and that's what he was doing, flexing his tits up and down and getting that blowjob, while Pleco Fez held his light meter up to the action. "Are we all ready?" he said.

"Will you come on?" said the girl.

"What's your name?"

"Fucking hell," she said. And she let go of me and walked over to Pleco Fez. She pointed in my direction. There was a moment's conference. And then they were all looking at me. Staci watched from her swing. The professionals stood aloof, with their massive swinging cocks. The girls watched me. The stage hands. Pleco Fez. They were all looking at me as I stood in that cold warehouse with my tiny cock. Pleco Fez pointed me to the door.

I was down at the Silver Dollar all the time after that. Days and nights. Unless I was working at the Jiffy Lube, which eventually I stopped. It was always somebody who would put a five into the jukebox. Then me and those college boys, we'd shoot stick all night. It was March and one of the boys had hit the keno machine for a hundred dollars. That sealed it and we fell to drinking. We'd been playing pool for hours, and my ass kept hurting me. But I couldn't remember why. Then I pulled that screwdriver out of my back pocket. They were standing across the table from me. Laughing. Looking cocky with their pool cues. I felt the heft of the tool. The ridges on the handle and the weight of the steel. It was a nice eight inches of screwdriver blade, which I tucked back into my pocket. I leaned across the felt. "One of you boys go buy me some more tequila," I said.

Around midnight we all stumbled drunk out of The Silver Dollar. Arm and arm, they held me like a battering ram against the crowd. Somebody opened the front door and we spilled into Railroad Street. They'd puked their guts, the both of them, right down the front of their shirts. Tripping, they let go of me, and I fell into the curb on my face.

Those college boys howled with glee. I was in the middle of a hiccup fit. There was blood in my teeth, and those boys, they just couldn't get enough of that. They were pretty drunk, but not near as drunk as me. We were in the parking lot by the side of the building, and they were standing over me in the darkness. One of the boys lit a smoke. He held out the pack. But as I pushed to my feet, reaching for a smoke, the little prick jerked the pack away, and they both thought that was really something.

So, I was like, "Give me your fucking money." And that really got them to laughing. I guess it was pretty funny. Me swaying on my feet. Choking back the hiccups. Blood on my chin. Nonetheless, I pulled the screwdriver out of my back pocket. I jabbed it at them. But they were quick on their feet, and one of them punched me in the face. The other kicked me, and I tripped over the curb, sprawling flat on the ground. The screwdriver clattered away, and they got down on top of me after that. One on my head. He twisted my arm behind my back, while the other one jerked my pockets inside out, spilling the last of my change, which they snatched off the pavement. And screaming with glee, they ran away into the night.

When they were gone, I rolled to my stomach. Then I lay on my back. There were clouds across the moon, glowing silver in the light. I stood up and collected my screwdriver. Then I slouched off in the direction of my mother's basement. My guts ached. My side. I had a tooth loose.

In the morning I pulled it from the gum and dug around in the bloody socket with my pinky finger. I wasn't welcome in The Dollar after that. But it was coming into springtime anyway, and the evenings were growing warm. It was just as good to get a pint of gin and go crawl out along the girders beneath the Higgins Street Bridge to the middle of the river. I'd carry my screwdriver out there and etch my thoughts into the iron. Above me the traffic roared on the concrete slabs of the bridge, while the moon glittered in the water below. Once the bottle was empty,

I'd lumber into the streets. I'd run into trees. I'd land in the doorway, and I'd sit in the alleys, listening to the lost fragments of voices, aching in the wind.

Somewhere in there I stopped showing up at my mother's. I took to sleeping fulltime at the campsite out in the river and eating what I could find from the dumpsters behind Safeway. I started to wander. I'd drift along the river at night. I'd walk into the hills by day. I used to wander up the side of Mount Sentinel overlooking Missoula. I sat up there in the breeze and watched the hang gliders cruising in the updrafts over the valley.

There was this great crowd of drunks down on Main Street one night, and a warm breeze had rolled out of the south. The drunks were surging together in their T-shirts and shorts. They shuffled like zombies through the orange glow of the street. The bars were letting out. I was on the corner asking people for money, and I kept dreaming about the smell of the greasy meat pouring out of The Ox. It was making my mouth water. And then once again, I saw Pleco Fez. He had one of the professionals with him. The mullet man. He looked tanned and blow-dried in a pink blazer and leather pants. They had a great story going between them. And they just couldn't get enough of themselves. The door to The Ox opened. Then Staci popped out between them. She was dressed in this metallic mini-dress. A little Star Trek number. And she was laughing these high, clear peels of belly laughter. They rang through the crowd like a church full of bells.

"Pleco Fez!" I yelled.

They all turned to look at me, where I stood with my shirt torn open. He had a pack of smokes in his hand, and he drew one out with his lips. The professional looked confused. His mouth hung open. Staci watched me. She had this distance in her eyes that was worse than spitting.

There were people everywhere. A truly incredible bunch of drunks. I planted myself on the sidewalk. I reached into my back pocket and I jerked out the screwdriver. I jabbed it at Pleco Fez, and said, "This is a mugging."

A few people had turned to notice. But Pleco Fez waved them off with a laugh. "You can't mug us in the middle of the street," he said.

"I can't get into another bar fight," said the professional.

"We're not in a bar," said Pleco Fez. "Relax."

"I've got a custody hearing," he said. He drew a couple of bills from his wallet.

"But this guy's a dill-hole," said Pleco Fez.

The professional held out the bills. "I'm not supposed to frequent bars," he said. "Come on. This is important. It's my kid, okay?"

Pleco Fez grimaced. It pained him greatly, but he too dug out his wallet. He pulled a few bills and gathered them together, along with the professional's money. He folded this into a neat little wad. Staci held a small clutch in her hands, but I could see pretty clearly that she had no intention of opening it. "Do you remember when we climbed up that signal tower?" I said.

She looked dreamy. She smiled. She was looking into a future that was very different from mine. "Take care of yourself," she said. There was a taxi waiting at the curb, and she packed herself into it. She slammed the door, and she folded her arms, and I could see her eyes were set straight ahead. She was dreamy and very pleased. Transcendent, I'd say. And I couldn't help but be just a little bit happy for her.

Pleco Fez threw his cigarette to the ground. He crushed it beneath his heel and held out the wad of bills. I reached for it, but he dropped the money. It lay on the sidewalk between my feet. The professional waved goodbye as though we were friends. Then they stepped into the taxi. "I really wanted to make it up to you," said Pleco Fez, as I scooped up the money. I tucked the bills into my pocket. Then I stood on the sidewalk with the screwdriver in my hand. People were watching me as I shuffled down Main toward the Clark Fork.

At the Bridge I walked down the bank to the water's edge. There I waded into the river in my pants and shoes. But as I got closer to my island, I saw a tiny flame sparking in the birch trees. It was a bunch of kids out there, high schoolers, I guess, and I could hear them laughing. Enraged, I started to run. I was crashing around in the water, struggling in my wet clothes. And when I came charging out of the water, flailing into the stones, they all scattered and ran. And when I crashed through the clearing, they were all but gone, snickering in the trees, as they splashed back across the river. They were in the water and they were wading for the shore. The little fucks. I could smell their weed. It was still pungent in the clearing.

And I cupped my hands and I yelled as loud as I could. "You little bastards stay off of my goddamn island!" I yelled. Then I squatted beneath my lean-to and I dug around in their dying coals with my screwdriver until a little finger of light flamed up in the ash.

The Nazi Method

I found Mother outside in the chaise lounge, watching a TV she'd strung through the window of the double-wide. Flopped next to her on the patio table sat a large-print book on Astral Projection and a couple of her favorite crystals. This big chunk of obsidian and a thick slab of quartz. She's getting up there, Mother. Complains about her veins, her arthritis. But she's got a sharp mind. Still crazy as ever for that off-brand religion. Stray prophets and ancient texts. Alien monuments on the surface of Mars. She was dressed in her usual stretch pants and flip-flops. Had on her T-shirt from the Worm Grunting Festival up in Sopchoppy. She was rubbing the crystals and going through the receipts from The Royal Palms. That's our motel. Or rather her motel. Which I manage.

"Aren't those our criminals?" she said, pointing at the TV. The screen showed grainy footage from a surveillance camera of two boys waving automatic pistols around a bank in Pensacola. "Maybe you ought to call the police."

"They checked out days ago," I said. Actually, they left in the middle of the night, having absolutely trashed our number 10 unit, down at the end of the motel.

"There was a fire fight," she said. "Killed a guard at the bank."

I popped the top off the beer I was holding and scratched my belly through my open shirt. It was one of Dad's old shirts, covered with Mai-

Tais and naked ladies.

Mother looked at her watch. She shot me this long, deadly stare over the beer.

"Amounts to the same thing," I said, "whether you get drunk alone, or you're the leader of nations. That's JP Sartre."

"You should have never gone to college," said Mother, "if that's all you were going to learn. Look at Rodger."

"The Cock-Doctor?" I said. My brother, the go-getter of the family. Skipping grades and getting scholarships. Now he's a plastic surgeon down in Boca Raton where he specializes in cocks. Claims he can find you another two inches in there.

"Don't be ugly," said Mother. "And speaking of those criminals, have you cleaned out unit 10 yet?"

We've got daily rates at The Royal Palms, or you can pay by the week or month. That's what these guys had done. They seemed all right when I first checked them in, but after a few weeks, this huge pile of garbage lay out front of unit 10. The Astroturf smelled of piss. They'd broken our patio furniture, ripped up the fence, and they'd tossed our pink flamingos into the scrubby junipers next to the Church's Fried Chicken. Then a few days ago they vanished. I'd only been in there once to plywood the window and stretch caution tape across the door. The unit was a total loss, littered with Sudafed boxes and spent cans of Drano. The whole property stunk of ammonia. "I don't think it's healthy in there," I said.

"Rodger says not to call the EPA," she said. "We'll never hear the end of it."

He was probably right about that, though I wasn't going to admit it. And, of course, that was another good reason not to get involved with the police.

I drained my beer and slouched off down the blacktop, flip-flops slapping against the soles of my feet. But I sure as hell wasn't going straight down to unit 10. A man my age who lives with his mother—

it's trench warfare. It's every goddamned yard. I had to let her watch me screw around for a bit. So I walked over to the bean-shaped pool, stooping to pull a few leaves from the water. Then I wandered out to Highway 98, where I stood beneath our sign, this royal palm tree, painted pink and circled with blinking marquee lights. I listened to them clicking as they made their revolutions. Through the trees I could see the sunlight shattering in the Gulf. I spent a few minutes picking trash out of a squat butterfly palm, and then I leaned against one of our tall sabals. A warm breeze blew against my skin, and I popped the last button on my naked ladies and Mai-Tais.

I watched this girl from unit 3 step out to the curb for a cigarette. Mostly we get retirees at The Royal Palms. Widows. Old ladies in muumuus, with accents out of Baltimore and Queens. Their husbands have worked hard all their lives, only to drop dead at the age of 64. Alone, they wander the flat white beaches of the Panhandle. Nothing but dog-eared paperbacks full of hot Latin love to pass around the pool. That wasn't the situation in unit 3.

She'd cropped her hair down short, dyed it blonde, and lacquered it stiff as plastic. Freckles spattered her cheeks, like something flicked off a spoon. She was thin as a cable whip, stringy-looking, and she was seriously pissed off. Beneath her cut-offs, I could see her legs were a mishmash of thick tattoos. None of it tourist stuff, dolphins and fairies. This girl had etched skulls and medieval crosses into her skin. Indecipherable phrases. Bizarre runes and coiled serpents. Mother must've checked her in, as I hadn't seen her before.

"Good afternoon," I said, walking along the units.

"What's so good about it?"

"I don't know," I said. "Maybe it's a piece of shit."

She considered me for a moment; then offered me her hand. The word FUCK was written across her knuckles. "Ellie," she said.

"Cecil Boggs."

And with a jerk she drew me close to her all of a sudden. Took a hold of me, like. I could feel her knobby breasts poking through her T-shirt. "You got any pills?" she said.

Now, I'm a forty-three year old man who lives with his mother in a double-wide trailer. So if there's one thing I understand it's the value of a negotiated settlement. "You're talking painkillers?" I said. My brother, the Cock-Doctor, had given his new wife a set of tits and a nose to mark the occasion of their recent nuptials, and they'd been up to see us for a couple of weeks so she could convalesce away from the prying eyes of the social set down in Boca Raton. Let the bruising fade and the stitches heal. Prescription bottles had been falling out of her pockets. It was after they left, that Mother had come across an ample stash of Oxycontin.

"How many you got?"

I looked back to where Mother sat watching the TV. She was rubbing the obsidian against the screen. It was Judge Judy on there, and I assumed she was trying to purge the evil out of one of the litigants. I turned back to her and said, "Why you got those numbers tattooed to your thighs?"

"It's my boyfriend's jersey number," she said. "He likes to call it out whenever he opens up my legs."

"Well, your boyfriend's a peckerwood," I said.

But she didn't find that amusing, even though it's in the script. We're supposed to bad mouth the boyfriend for a while, her and I. Establish ourselves simpatico. But she just looked away, her chin dimpled up, and her face got all blotchy. I could see that she was about to cry, and so I got kind of dejected about the whole conversation. "Maybe this isn't such a good idea," I said.

Ellie smiled, but her eyes remained hard. She stared into the distant gulf. "Yeah," she said. She slipped back through the door. "He's a peckerwood all right."

And then I was left standing on the curb in the blazing sun. I could smell the water on the hot breeze. I could smell the exhaust from the cars on 98, and I felt very alone in the world right then. More alone than I could remember feeling in years. It just came to me right out of the sky. Just like that woman up in Alabama who got smacked with that meteor. It just slapped me all of a sudden. And I realized that I had not spoken conversationally to anyone—I mean besides Mother and the Cock-Doctor—for going on a year.

Except maybe the widows.

That night, I was in the kitchen with Mother getting the shrimp ready to boil. I'd bought these fat whites, fresh out of the Gulf with their heads still on them. Mother groaned, pulling a skillet of corn bread out of the oven. She had her crystals with her and the book open on the counter beside the sink. It was after Daddy left us that she got into that weirdness, going to all the conventions and the group retreats. She met the fellow space cadets out there. And she'd drag them back to The Royal Palms. About a half dozen over the years. This last one had dressed in long white robes. He'd shaved his skull, and he had kept a little red dot on his forehead, like an alien. This was the guy who brought us the crystals. He said they represented the duality of the human soul. Good and evil. Life and death. He said you could live forever if you just focused on the quartz within your mind and flushed all the obsidian out of your body. Mother liked him the most out of all of them. But then one day he too hitched a ride on a moonbeam, and just like Daddy we never saw him again. They'd come and they'd go. But what about me, I used to wonder. Where's my spaceship come to blast me off of this coast?

"These crystals represent the duality of the human soul," said Mother.

"I know they do, Mother," I said. I dumped the shrimp into the boil. She covered the corn bread and stirred the lima beans. I took a cold can of beer from the cooler.

"So, you make any progress on unit 10?"

"I think we're going to need to call in the professionals," I said.

"Rodger says that's a bad idea."

"Well the Cock-Doctor is a jackass," I said. But I knew as well as he did what would happen if I called in the professionals. We'd end up with a whole squad of environmental engineers descending on The Royal Palms with fistfuls of exposure charts and regulation manuals. I could see the beakers full of ground water. The test tubes full of dirt. We'd need haz-mat certified contractors. Men dressed like astronauts. They'd shut us down at the height of the season, wandering the blacktop in their bunny suits and oxygen. "You know," I said—this was my angle—"the problem for me is mostly the headaches. The ammonia hurts my sinuses. You remember those pills Rodger left here last month? If you were to give me some of those pills, I think I could bear it."

"That's a controlled substance," said Mother. "It's dangerous, and I'm giving those pills back to Rodger next time he's here."

"They're not dangerous," I said. "There's whole bureaucracies of the US government whose purview is to ensure their safety."

"They're only to be taken under a doctor's care," she said. "What if you ODed?" She tapped herself in the chest. "I'd be on the hook for it legally."

"No you wouldn't," I said. "You could just tell the police that I found them. You'd say it was the Cock-Doctor's fault."

"I wish you would stop calling your brother that."

"Rodger," I said. "You could blame it on Rodger."

"Fine," she said. "I'll give you one pill."

"I'm going to need more than one."

"I'll think about it," she said. "Make good progress and maybe I'll give you more."

"Just tell me where you put the bottle."

"No," she said. "Absolutely not." She pointed to my boil. "Shrimp's ready."

When I stepped outside the next morning I could smell the water. I could hear the gulf rolling in the quiet air. To the east the sky looked pink with the sunrise. I walked through the sand and the grass to the side of the double-wide where I stopped to take a piss in the junipers. The world seemed calm and empty. When I came back to the pool, I saw Ellie sitting on the curb in front of unit 3. She had been crying, I think, and her face looked splotchy around the cheeks, but she composed herself as I approached. I took the pill Mother had given me out my pocket. Smiling, I held it like a diamond in the morning light.

Her face burst with pleasure for an instant, then clouded over. "Just one?"

"I've got to clean out that unit," I said, pointing toward number 10. "Then I'll get more."

"The meth lab?" she said. She touched her nose. "I can smell it."

"That's right," I said. "The meth lab."

"Tell you what," she said. "You give me that pill and I'll help you." She was smiling now, wiping the tears from her cheeks. Standing, she held out her hand.

"Like a down payment," I said.

"Sure," she said, looking into the scattered palms. "Like a down payment."

I placed the pill in her hand. I thought she'd dry swallow it on the spot. Instead she shoved it into the pocket of her cut-offs. "Let me get my stuff," I said.

A few minutes later I rolled up to unit 10 with a wheelbarrow full of cleaning supplies. I had Comet and dish soap. I had rags and scrubbies, a bucket of water, rubber gloves and a toilet brush. I had a ball-peen hammer and a pry-bar. Ellie was already waiting outside, dressed in a set of baggy mechanic's coveralls. I pulled away the caution tape. It ripped easily, and fluttered across the blacktop into the pool. I took out my thick ring of keys.

Inside, there was a smell like sugar and cat shit. But it wasn't just the chemical stench of the sludge buckets in the kitchenette. They had broken out the window in the bathroom and a possum had gotten inside and died. There were flies everywhere. Piles of Sudafed boxes heaped on the floor. I could smell the Drano soaked into the carpets. On the coffee table sat two Coleman fuel canisters and a cardboard box full of gutted 12-volt batteries. There was a rusty tank of ammonia next to the bed and another of hydrogen chloride leaning against the wall. I pushed at the box of dead batteries with my toe.

"Nazi method," said Ellie. She pointed at the batteries. Our eyes were burning, and I could see Ellie wiping back tears.

"You're telling me Nazis did this?" I felt sick and dizzy.

"It's just the name," she said. She went into the bathroom.

"What do you know about it?" I said as I followed.

There was daylight in the windows; shafts of dust stood in the mounds of garbage. My head was full of snot and slobber from the ammonia. But I followed her, watching as she opened the medicine cabinet, the drawers. She lifted the lid on the commode tank. Next to the sink lay a blackened spoon and a lighter, a bag of cotton wads, and a hypodermic. But there were no drugs to be found, and she had begun to sob again. These great heaves caught in her chest, and I could see her wince from the pain. I thought maybe to reach out and touch her, but I didn't. I just stood listening to her cry. After a moment, she stopped. She seemed to buck herself up. "I don't know much about it," she said. "My brother makes it. He's—yeah. Look… let's just get to work, okay?"

"What's the matter?" I said. I followed her back to the kitchenette.

"Nothing," she said. "What's the matter with you?"

"All kind of shit's the matter with me," I said. "But I'm not the one cries all the time."

"So, you're one of those," she said. "I guess now you'll want to tell me all of your problems, right? Go ahead. It's part of the service. But keep working."

So I did. I told her all about Mother and the Cock-Doctor while we cleaned. All through the day we piled up the garbage. The cardboard and the canisters. We threw it outside to the Astroturf. We mustered the sludge buckets together in the kitchenette, and we rolled the tanks into the bathroom. Me talking. Then we scrubbed the walls, the counters. We pulled up the carpet. We hurled the mattress out the front door. I told her my life's story. I told her about flunking out of college, and I told her about the women I'd known. How I used to fall into orbit around some girl, and wind up in Key West or Biloxi. Wherever it was her daddy owned a bar or a restaurant or a fishing boat. Anything I could weld or hammer, pour into a glass or fry up in a pan. I told her about my boy in Jacksonville. He's got be in the sixth grade about now, and how his mother used to let him call me around my birthday for a while. But he's given it up now. She's married again. And I guess this new fellow's a pretty good father, as far as fathers go. "I don't think he hits the kid," I said. "That's about all you can ever ask out of a father."

"And why do you live with your mother?"

"About every six months I wind up back here," I said. "I can install a toilet, and I can lay fresh carpet. The widows don't give me a hard time and I keep the units in good order. In the afternoons, I like to float in the pool with a cold can of beer."

"That doesn't sound so bad," she said.

We were in the bathroom. I looked out through the window, into the jungle beyond our property. "I guess not," I said.

"Well, if you're so miserable about your life then change," she said. "Go get a job chopping cocks like your brother. He's got a wife, right?"

"Three of them," I said. "Builds 'em up out of scrap titties. And he don't chop cocks, he porks 'em out."

So we got to laughing about that for a while, and I guess we were having a pretty okay time together working on the unit and trying not to gag on the fumes. But eventually it got to be too much for us, and I noticed that Ellie hadn't spoken in a while. I went through the unit and found her in the kitchenette, where she'd gone quite green in the face. So, I pointed her to the exit, where we both staggered outside, our eyes and noses pouring out of our heads. Ellie fell to her knees. She vomited into the sand. I was squatting on the pavement, feeling no better. Dizzy and sick. I rolled to my back, and I stared into the sky. The clouds looked watery through my burning eyes. I could barely breathe. After a moment, I too rolled to my stomach and threw up. Ellie lay flopped in the sand next to me, a sprawl of gangly limbs. She stretched her legs, long and skinny, and I could feel them against my own. There was a gentle wind, and she put her hands behind her head. I pushed myself to my elbow and looked down at her. The shadows of the butterfly palms played across her skin. She was a very pretty girl, beneath all the ink. It's not that I'm opposed to tattoos. It's just that hers were brutal-looking, heavy and crude. She looked up at me in the silence, probing my face. "You don't like them, do you?" she said.

"I don't mind them."

"No, they're ugly," she said. "I know they are. My boyfriend's getting better. But he learnt on me. I've got good ones too, though." And then she stood. She unzipped her mechanic's coveralls and pulled the zipper down past her breasts, where the coils of two ancient looking sea creatures spiraled around her nipples. Intricately scaled. Blue-green and shimmering. They were living things, thriving. Winding through the murk and silence. Even on her pale skin I could see them in the cold, lunar blackness of the great deep. She had begun to cry again, and big tears rolled down her freckled cheeks. For a moment I was speechless. Then I looked away, watching a flock of pelicans gliding east towards Eglin. There were gulls turning arcs over the water. I sat forward and stumbled to my feet.

"You hear about that bank job?" I said. "It was these boys who had rented this room, you know it? I saw them on TV."

She zipped up her coveralls. "Did you call the police?"

"Not yet," I said.

"Why not?"

"I don't want the hassle of it."

"I heard there was a man killed at the bank," she said. "Doesn't that matter to you?"

"Sure," I said. "But—"

"Well, it matters to me," she said. She began to sob again, and she buried her face in her hands.

"What do you know about it?" I said. "Was it your boyfriend? Your brother?"

She steeled herself, closed her eyes. And when she opened them, she looked dead on at the door to unit 10. "Are they here?" I said, pointing down towards unit 3. "Are they hiding out in your room?"

"No," she said. Then, "Come on. Let's get to work." She pushed back into the room.

"Wait," I said. But I said it under my breath, and she made no move to stop. She marched into the unit and began tossing carpet fragments out the door. I stood by the curb for a moment. But then I joined her, and we worked in silence after that, all through the afternoon. I was feeling highly conflicted about it. And I had a lot of fear too, but I can't pretend that I did not want to see those coiled beasts one more time.

That evening I found Mother at the patio table watching Idol. She had her crystals. She was tapping the quartz, rubbing the obsidian. There was some boy singing on the TV, and I suppose she must've been pulling for him through the crystals.

"I cleaned out the unit," I said. "You told me I could have more pills when I finished."

"You see they caught one of the criminals?"

I shot a glance down toward Ellie's unit. "How about those pills," I said.

"What about them?"

"You promised me the bottle when I finished."

"The bottle?" Mother set her crystals aside. "What do you need the whole bottle for?"

"We had a deal," I said. "Clean the unit, get the bottle."

"We had no deal," she said. "I told you maybe."

"Mother, you said—"

"I said no such thing." She stood, gathered up the TV, and stalked into the trailer. I was left alone in the silence of her wake. I took her crystals from the patio table, fingered them a moment. Then, I slipped them into my pocket. After a while I headed over to our sign, where I squatted to watch the road. It was quiet, and I could hear the gulf beyond the highway. The door to unit 10 was wide open, airing out. I was going to need a truck to haul off those buckets of sludge in the morning. It's hard not to wonder sometimes if that's all life ever amounts to. Maybe it's all just toxic goo to be moved from one side of town to the other.

I was thinking these things, with my hands shoved into my pockets, holding Mother's crystals and watching the sky mellow into the west. And it was only this faint rumble at first, some plane taking off from Eglin. They come in low over the trees, these fat, wide-bodied military jets, transports, and fighters. I've even seen The President himself, that massive 747 of his, flanked by four deafening F-16s. He'll come rolling over the pines, about a thousand feet off the deck. Maybe I'm out by the pool, clearing leaves or picking up litter. Just me and the widows. We'll look up, gap-faced and stupid, watching in unison as that tight wedge climbs over the gulf, like the winged chariot of some Bronze Age god. I glanced up, half expecting to see the President now, but it was just some routine C-130.

Another of the lesser imps. Like me. And I let out this long breath of air, which I think perhaps I had been holding onto for all of my life. I shut my eyes and breathed.

"It is a night for us lesser imps," I said.

Ellie scowled when I gave her the news. She looked bitter. Her face twisted, and she began to tremble, to hyperventilate. Her sobs broke out in long, jagged wails. Then she bore down on her jaws. She clenched up. She just couldn't take it anymore, and her face screwed down tight. She was gripping a scream. An explosion. There was some final supernova of pure rage stuck in her chest. And she balled up her fist, and she punched me as hard as she could. I dodged a second blow. A third. And I caught her wrists after that. I twisted her away from me.

"I'm sorry," I said.

"You pathetic piece of shit!" she said.

"Look, I'm kind of thinking this is a bad idea, anyway," I said. "I know I owe you something, though. Maybe I can come up with fifty dollars."

"A bad idea?" she said. "You're thinking this is a bad idea?"

"To be honest, I don't even know if I could," I said.

She stepped towards me, unzipping her coveralls. I was rooted to the spot, unable to move, and she grabbed my hands and pulled me to her breasts. I cupped my palms around them, sticky with sweat from the work we'd done. I could feel the hard knots of her nipples between my fingers. Her heart was crashing in her ribs. I could feel such a heat coming out of her. I don't know what I had expected, something cold as eels, a corpse girl, a ghoul. Something that had crawled up out of the ground. But it was this heat that seemed to come pouring out of her, pouring right out between my fingers. All that heat. And I jumped back. I stumbled down the curb. "I don't need fifty dollars," she said. "I need pills. That old lady's got them."

I was staring at my out-turned palms as though they leapt with flame. "You know they caught one of those boys," I said. "I bet the Sheriff's putting the screws to him right now to find the other one."

"I reckon," she said. I glanced up to see the thin line of her lips.

"Where are we supposed to do it?" I said. "In here? Are we going to be alone?"

She didn't move, didn't jerk a muscle. Not the slightest flicker of her eyes. She just stared into me, standing with my palms out, like some dejected Lazarus by the side of the road. "We'll find a place to do it," she said. "Are you going to get me those pills or not?"

I came into Mother's room and sat on the edge of the bed. She had a copy of *Dianetics* cracked open on the blanket beside her and a pile of junk mail from various institutes and retreats. She had pamphlets on Tarot and channeling, another on the spaceship landing about to go down in Colorado. Some group wanted donations to build a saucer-friendly space-pad. She had her candles lit, her incense. She'd plopped the TV onto the corner of the dresser at the foot of the bed, and it was tuned to a show on witches. I patted her shin. She took her glasses off her nose, regarding me with that familiar contempt. But I wasn't taking it this time. I rolled off the bed and shuffled through the pile of clothes on the floor. I forced my way to the closet where she kept the moth-balled steamer truck full of Daddy's old things. Squatting, I pushed open the lid, and from the trunk, I pulled out a couple of his Hawaiian shirts. His woodies and sand dunes. His big parrots and droopy tulips. I could still smell his tobacco and Aqua Velva. Sitting cross-legged, I pulled off my flip-flop and held it against the bottom of a shoe. In my mind he was a man who could take the moon in his fingers and blow it like a ball of dandelion seed. Thus it amazed me to find that the size of our feet had now converged into one. He'd been my age, I think, when he left us.

"Why don't you throw all this shit out?" I said.

"Did you grab my crystals?" said Mother.

"I asked you a question," I said. "Why don't you sell this godforsaken place and move down to Boca Raton with Rodger?"

"I wouldn't ever do that to you," she said. "Did you grab my crystals?"

"I might've," I said. "Tell you what. I'll swap you for the bottle."

"It's no good," she said. "I called Rodger and he told me not to let you near those pills and to flush them down the commode. You are now free of them, Cecil."

I shut my eyes. "Goddamnit, Mother," I said.

"I'd like my crystals back," she said.

"It's no good," I said. "I called Pluto and they said not to let you near those crystals and to hurl them into the gulf. You are now free of them, Mother."

"You did no such thing," she said.

"I sure did," I told her.

When Ellie saw my face, she could tell I'd come up empty. I thought she'd yell at me again. And I got ready for her to smack me one. But in fact she just began to sob. She put her forehead to the concrete and banged it once. Then again, harder. And a third. "Stop that," I said.

She sank along the wall to the ground, where she sat cross-legged against the door, weeping and grinding her teeth. I could see her face flush with blood. And she began to hit the concrete with her fist. "I just don't know what to do," she said. I squatted and tried to take her hand, but she pulled free and pushed me away. When she spoke she sounded vague. Fading. She was fading out. "You ought to just go," she said. And standing, she slipped back through the door. It clicked between us, and I was left sitting on the curb.

"Open up a minute," I called.

"If you knew what was good for you," she said. "You'd get a million miles away."

"It's that boyfriend of yours, isn't it?" I said. I banged on the door. "If he's in there, I'm going to call the police." I kept banging, but she wouldn't return. "I can get through this door," I said. "I've got the damned key."

I took out my keys and I flipped through them. I looked at the door, then around at the pool, the other units. Nothing stirred. I could see the TVs glowing in the windows all along the motel. I put the key in the lock and that roused her. I heard footfalls on the linoleum. The weight of her body settled against the door. "You better not come in here," she said. I could feel the tumblers against the prongs on the key, but I didn't twist it. If he was in there. Hiding out. Armed. Well, then opening that door would be the culminating act in this grand pageant of idiocy called my life.

I pulled the key out and walked along the sidewalk to the road. I could ignore it all, I thought—it wasn't my problem. Or I could call the police, that's what the Cock-Doctor would do. I had reason to suspect that a murderer was holed up at the motel. It was my civic duty to call someone. But I felt unmoored. It was as if I'd stopped somehow, while all around me the great flood of suffering that is our life together had continued to roll across the surface of this sad little ball. Me and Ellie. My mother. Our roadside motel.

So, I marched back to Ellie's unit. I jabbed the key into the lock. I twisted and pushed through. I jumped back, expecting he'd fire off a couple of slugs into the night. Nothing. Then I peeked around the frame. Ellie sat in the bed. She was on her knees sobbing with her face in her hands. I went inside, and the door slammed shut behind me. I was about to speak, but then I jerked to a stop and dropped the keys. It was him in there all right. One of the damned meth-heads from unit 10. He was laid in the bed. Ellie glared but said nothing. She only cried. And I was gagging, holding my mouth in my hands. For it was truly an incredible amount of blood. A smell like wet iron. On the linoleum in the kitchenette. Such an incredible smear across the floor. And my heart kicked over. Pain jabbed in my chest. We've had guests die on us a couple of times. There was this frat kid once who drank himself to death. And this old man had suffered a heart attack out by the pool. Those deaths were both messy, vomit and shit. But this was on a whole new level. Blood had soaked into the carpet. It saturated the blankets and the mattress. But he looked peaceful, this boy. He lay with his arms by his sides. I felt my eye twitch and my vision tunnel. I knew I needed to sit down or to squat or to get outside into the air, and I put my hand to the back of the chair to steady myself.

"What the hell?" I said. The boy's eyes popped open. Ellie took his head into her lap. She began to stroke his temples, wiping at the sweat with a washcloth. I couldn't breathe. I kept gasping these ragged gulps of foul air. Slowly I sank to my knees.

He was naked to the waist. All but hairless with big muscles. And he was covered in tattoos. A lion's head. An eagle in flight. An electric guitar. On his ribs, I saw the face of a girl. Spider webs and Celtic knots covered his legs. I don't think he was watching me. I don't know how much consciousness he even had. Dreamy, soupy. I could see his lips move but no words came from them. He'd been shot in the stomach, a shotgun probably. The skin had sucked back upon itself, and these little red sphincters had bloomed around the ugly black pits. When he breathed, I could see blood bubbling in one of the holes.

"He's got a Viking ship on his back," said Ellie. She could see that I was looking at his tattoos. They exchanged a long, silent stare between themselves. I touched the lion on his chest. He glared at me.

"He's your boyfriend?"

She shook her head. "My brother," she said. "It was that fucker who shot him."

"The one they're putting the screws to down at the sheriff's department," I said.

Ellie nodded. "I just need to give him something," she said.

"Mother flushed the pills," I said. "I'm not lying."

Ellie bit her lip. She held her brother's fingers. "You stupid son-of-a-bitch," she said, pounding him on the chest. "What the fuck were you thinking?" There were tears in the boy's eyes.

"He needs to get to a hospital," I said. "He'll die like this."

"He'll die anyway," she said. I looked at the boy's eyes as she said it, but I could read nothing in them, though it was probably true what she said, with his guts all shot up like that. "I just can't stand to see him in pain," she said. "He's my little baby brother."

Tears streamed down her face. She was shaking as she stroked his temples. He moved his head as if to look away.

"A man's dead," I said. "Down at the bank."

"I know it," she said. "You think I don't know it? He probably had a sister too."

"A mother," I said. "Maybe a little boy of his own."

"Will you just shut up," she said. "I know it already."

I was standing above him, thinking to myself that he deserved this. I was thinking that it was some kind of justice. But at the same time I could not help but feel a deep pity for him, and a sympathy, which I do not believe I have ever felt for anyone before. He was such a damned waste of humanity, too. This thing. I shouldn't feel it. It was supposed to be contempt that I felt and righteousness even. He'd killed a man. His eyes darted between us but he made no sound. He just looked at us with these big, glassy marbles in his head. "Come on," said Ellie. "Please, just help him."

"I don't have anything," I said. I reached into my pockets to turn them inside out. A gesture of proof. But when I opened my hands, I held Mother's crystals, one in each of my palms. Ellie took them. "What the hell are these?" she said.

"Mother's crystals."

"What are they for?"

"Good and evil," I said.

"This is the good one," she said, holding up the quartz. I looked at them in her fingers. They were very pretty to look at, the crystals, with flecks of red in the scalloped surface of the obsidian. The quartz was shot through with milky thunderheads. Tiny rainbows glinted off the facets. I wished Rodger was there. He'd have taken over the situation. Done what had to be done. I merely felt sick.

"No," I said, pointing at the crystals. "It's not a matter of a good one and a bad one. It's just a matter of difference. That's actually what Mother doesn't understand about them."

"What do you do with them?" she said.

I scratched my head. I looked from the crystals to the boy, to the blood seeping from his holes. I didn't know at all what to do with them, but I took them into my hands and I touched them to each of his wounds. I rubbed them in little circular motions, the way I'd seen Mother rub them. Then, after I had touched every wound, I placed both crystals on the boy's forehead. He closed his eyes. I looked at Ellie and she nodded, and I took her hand in mine and I placed it over the boy's nose. Then I pinched her fingers together, and I set my hand over his mouth. We could feel him trying to breathe in quick, shallow jerks for a bit. But it didn't last. And after a moment he lay still. That was all there was to it. Ellie took the crystals from off his forehead, and she slipped them into her pocket.

We stood together watching the corpse on the bed for a while. Might've been twenty minutes we stood there. Ellie didn't cry after that. She was just breathing. I could see something bitter pinching at the corners of her mouth, but she'd gone numb I think. Gone. Finally, she turned and walked out the door. I followed her to the curb, where she went first to her car. But then she thought better of that and just started walking. She stopped though, in the middle of the parking lot, and she turned to look at me one last time. She stood motionless, watching me. I think she wanted to say something. I sat on the curb. I let my hands dangle between my knees. I knew I'd have to call the police in a minute, but for a while longer I could rest in the silence of the night air. Then she turned and walked onto the highway. I listened to the bugs, the cars. Out beyond the dunes, I could hear the rolling waters of the unfathomable gulf.

Cerrito Blanco

All that week Tessa had watched the gas station from their trailer behind the Rio Chama Steakhouse, where her father had taken the new job. The gas station sat across the highway next to Carla's Diner. There was an adobe church up the hill, and a dirt road that wound through the trailers and boxy houses. Goats had eaten the fields bare of grass. Beyond the river, thick cottonwoods grew along the base of a crumbling ridge that overlooked the town of Cerrito Blanco and the Rio Chama Valley. Her father sat on a hay bale in the yard. He wore his houndstooth toque and white chef's smock. He was smoking a cigarette, which he had promised not to do in the trailer. Up at the steakhouse, the day cooks had finished the lunch rush, and she could still smell grilling meat and burning sage.

"I thought we were going to Bandolier," said Tessa.

"But now it turns out I have to work," he said. He dropped his cigarette into a dead beer can and pointed into the rocky field of stubby junipers and buffalo grass. "There're dinosaur bones out there," he said. "Why don't you find us a T. Rex, and we'll retire to Maui."

The air felt hot on her cheeks. Tessa could smell the river and the New Mexico desert, sage and dirt. "I wish Mom was here," she said. Her mother was a raw nerve with him, and she had taken to plucking at it every now and again. "Mom would take me."

He didn't reply, though after a moment he wiped his thumb across his cheek.

"If we lived with Grandmother in Denver then I could see her again," said Tessa.

"You're never going to see that woman," he said.

"She apologized," said Tessa.

"Your mother shot me," he said.

"Grandmother said you deserved it."

Leonard clenched his fists in rage. The vein in his forehead had become prominent, and she began to wonder if he would hit her someday. Had he ever hit her mother, Darcy? Darcy always said to leave a man that hit you. She said you have to push them right to the brink of it, but you don't ever let them cross the line. "Did you ever hit her?" she said. "Is that why you deserved it?"

"No, I never hit her," said Leonard. Twisting, he lifted his smock to reveal the pink pucker of flesh beneath his ribs. He touched it gingerly, but it was only dead scar. "You are the meanest little child. The woman shoots me, and now you want me to go live with her mother."

There were tears on his face, and Tessa had begun to cry, too. She always felt awful afterwards and hated herself for it. She felt the patchy spots of hair where he'd run the clippers over her head. "Can I at least go to the gas station?" she said.

"Not by yourself," he said. "Tomorrow, I promise we'll go to Bandolier."

"We should just go back to Denver," she said.

"Your mother can rot in that jail," he said. He shook himself to his feet and stomped off toward the steakhouse.

"I will see her again," Tessa called. "She'll get out in three years. Five at the most."

θ

Leonard came out to the dumpster to smoke a cigarette and stew about his daughter. He squatted in the shade of a stack of milk crates. He'd chopped the octopus for the ceviche, sliced the calamari into rings, and put the tamales on to steam. All he had left were the stuffed jalapeños. Those little poppers went down perfectly with a flight of tequilas and a cold glass of beer. That's what had done it for the hostess back at O'Malley's in Denver. Thank God the pistol he had bought for Darcy's birthday had been a cheap piece of shit. If it hadn't jammed after the first shot, he'd now have that hostess's death on his conscience as well.

Jim Tressel came out of the kitchen in his snake skin boots and faded Levis. He stood by the backdoor, kicking at the chunks of gravel. On his belt, he wore a massive, silver buckle inlaid with a golden cow skull. His silk shirt hung loose around his neck, and he held a set of tongs and a hotel pan full of steaks. They had been good friends, back in their days at CIA—the culinary institute, not the intelligence agency. That was a long time ago, but as soon as Jim heard that Leonard had gotten fired, he had offered him this job down in New Mexico at the steakhouse. He was a friend in need, because it wasn't merely that Leonard had gotten caught with a hostess in the walk-in. While that looks bad on a resumé, it's hardly irreparable. But it was his wife who had caught them, the head-waitress at O'Malley's. And getting shot by his wife and then stumbling through the dining room and out to the street, that's what put him on the blacklist in Denver. It was times like that, Leonard figured, you saw who your true friends were. Jim set the hotel pan on the lip of the dumpster. With his tongs he lifted a thick porterhouse and dropped it into the garbage. There were a half-dozen such steaks, as well as five New York strips and about four pounds of uncut tenderloin in the pan. Leonard struggled to his feet, while Jim upended the tray. The meat slid off with a plop.

"Damn that woman," Jim said. "You know, she worked for me three years before she opened up Carla's? Why couldn't she go down to Española?"

On the phone Jim had painted a rosier picture of the Rio Chama

Steakhouse so far as the financials were concerned. However, it seemed the tourist trade along Highway 84 couldn't support two restaurants in Cerrito Blanco. "We could revamp the appetizers," said Leonard. "At O'Malley's we did these little numbers with artichoke hearts and quail eggs. We need to—"

"We need to get serious," said Jim.

"Get serious?" The pile of wet meat lay flopped together on the bags of garbage.

"I can't afford to keep throwing out steaks," said Jim. "If business doesn't pick up soon I'm going to have to let someone go. You understand what I'm saying?"

"Not exactly," said Leonard.

"What I mean is, something needs to happen."

"Something has to happen?"

"You ever pull off an electrical meter?" said Jim. He took a set of wire cutters from his back pocket and laid them on the lip of the dumpster. "You just cut the tamper tag," he said. "That's about all there is to it."

"That and 200 amps," said Leonard.

Jim grinned. "You'll want to be careful," he said, "and not short out the meter housing."

"The power company will just replace it," said Leonard. "Couple days, maybe."

"And then we do it again," said Jim. He tucked the hotel pan under his arm and turned to leave. "I'd hate to have to let anybody go is all."

Leonard picked up the wire cutters. He pulled his toque off his head and wiped his face. He felt the tightness in his side. It'd go days without hurting and then stiffen up. He'd get these sharp jabs running through his gut. He thought about the blood and the bile and the screams of the hostess in his arms. Through the smoke, he had looked at Darcy. The pistol clicked, and that was the last time he had looked her in the eyes. It clicked again. Then she threw it at him, and the images grew vague.

He must have crashed through the dining room. He could remember the sidewalk and the squad cars.

Leonard had always sensed the presence of that mythical highway in the American consciousness, the one that runs through mountain passes and painted deserts and then drains into the setting suns of a place like San Diego. Maybe they were just words on the radios in the dish rooms of the restaurants, but when he was a young man, Leonard had dreamed of being a rock star chef in some fusion steakhouse out in Beverly Hills. He'd rub shoulders with Mick Jagger and Magic Johnson. They'd feature his cookbooks on the *Today Show*. But that was all smoke and dreams. He only had maybe a dollar in his pocket but Jim owed him for the week. That might get them back to Darcy's mother in Denver, and a feeling like cold steel crept up his guts when he thought about that.

He held the cutters up to the blazing sky. Squinting through the opened jaws, he snipped them back and forth, as though he meant to clip the wires off the sun.

θ

Tessa had been in the field near the steakhouse, but after a while, she had walked along the arroyo and then down to the highway, where shreds of cellophane blew in the hot wind. The sun had burned her cheeks, her arms. Her shoulders were pink around the straps of her tank top. Waves of heat rolled off the asphalt in the distance. Her throat burned from the dust. Dust covered her face, her legs. She crossed the road to the gas station, where the sign claimed they had ice-cold Coca-Cola, though Tessa had no money to buy one. On the road, tourists zipped past. They were hauling their boats out to the reservoir. Some headed south to the casinos near Española and the past-life therapy centers down in Santa Fe. If they stopped, it was to fill their cars at the gas station, their minivans and RVs, or to lunch at one of the restaurants. Indeed, somebody had parked a BMW slantwise at Carla's. That's where she saw the boy. He stood under the shadow of the eaves at the diner. He had thick, black hair that hung down shaggy around his face. He was a small boy. Skinny. Though not as skinny as she, and it was hard to tell, but she felt that he was probably younger. Eleven, maybe. "There's a dog in that BMW," he said.

Tessa looked across the road to the steakhouse.

"Well, it's a fucking hot day," he said. "Don't you think?"

She folded her gawky arms and squinted. Heat shimmered off the roof of the BMW. Nodding, she walked to the car and peered into the backseat, where she saw the dog. It lay panting at one of the windows. Its tongue had lolled out of its mouth, and its eyes were glazy in the heat. She looked up the dirt road at the scattered trailers, the adobe church. Near a fence post at the corner of the field lay several chunks of concrete, and the land was dotted with junipers and cholla cactus. "You live around here?" she said.

He pointed to a trailer off to the side of Carla's. "I think the guy's in the diner," he said. "But you tell him. My mom doesn't want me bugging the customers."

"Go fill a bowl with water," she said.

"Are you going to tell him?"

"No."

"What are you going to do?"

"I'm a get this dog out of there."

"But you could just go tell them," he said.

"But then he wouldn't learn a damned thing now, would he?"

The boy ran for the trailer. At the fence, Tessa kicked at the chunks of concrete until she found the biggest one she could lift. Squatting she heaved it to her chest. She stood and tottered with it, and stumbled through the gravel back to the BMW. It was this great slab of concrete, she held. The jagged edges dug into her arms and the cement flaked off on her skin. She was waiting for the boy, and when he stepped out the trailer, he held a pot in his arms. Water splashed over the sides as he ran through the parking lot and along the windows at the front of the diner, the idea struck Tessa that this might not be the best route, but it was all happening very fast now. The mechanisms were in place. Suddenly, it had taken on a soul of its own.

She didn't want to drop the chunk on the dog's head or to shatter the glass into the back seat, so she went to the driver's side. There, she took a step back to build momentum. Then, with a grunt she heaved the slab into the window. The glass shattered with a blast of tiny cubes. The shards exploded and flashed in the sun. The car alarm squawked, and Tessa pulled the lock. She jerked the handle on the backseat, and grabbing the dog by the collar, she dragged it to the ground. It was a short-haired dog, stocky and pug-nosed. The boy set the water down. Tessa scanned the fields, the goats, and the cottonwoods growing along the river. A line of cars stretched out along the highway, but the car's alarm drowned out every other possible sound.

"We better run," she said.

"My name's Hector," said the boy.

"Tessa," she said.

θ

Leonard stood in the parking lot at Carla's Diner. He could hear the man screaming inside, this big tourist. He had a voice that rolled out of the gut. Domination by sheer volume. Leonard squatted beside the BMW. He peeled a little fractured glass off the broken edge of the window. On the floorboards lay a massive chunk of concrete. Glass lay on the ground, glinting in the sun. There was glass across the seats, and someone had left a pot of water near the back tire. The vanity plates on the car read "Buck7," which implied the existence of six other Bucks from the state of Michigan. Leonard scratched his stubby face. He could feel the wire cutters stuffed into the back pocket of his pants. He looked at the meter on the side of the building. In the diner, he could see the tourist—this Buck—standing at the counter with his hands planted on the Formica top. He was tall and thick, a kind of slab-gutted ex-athlete, dressed in a pink Izod and blue shorts. He kept pointing at the woman. Leonard guessed it was Carla. She leaned in the pass-through, this chunky woman with a round face. Her black hair had fallen from the knot at the top of her head. Steam from the dishwasher rolled in the air.

He took the wire cutters out of his pocket. He had meant only to scout around, get the lay of the land. He would return that night under the cover of darkness. Then again, perhaps this was the perfect opportunity. Power lines ran from the pole at the road to the side of the building. He could see the tamper tag hanging from the bottom of the meter housing. In the restaurant, Buck had a grip on one of the stools, as though he meant to rip it from the floor. There was a jukebox and a defunct cigarette machine. A corkboard on the wall held scrawled signs stuck on it at odd angles. Buck had begun to pound his fist on the counter. Leonard looked to the steakhouse across the highway. He peeled more glass from the jagged edge of the window. Buck was pacing in the diner, and Leonard closed his eyes. He stood, dropping the crumbled glass. He stuffed the wire cutters back into his pocket and pushed through the doors into the cool interior of the restaurant.

"I saw your boy running," said Buck. He smiled when he saw Leonard, as if he guessed immediately that Leonard was on his side. They were two white men, after all, confronting an Indian about her delinquent son. "I know he did it and I know he's your boy."

"You better leave," said Leonard.

Buck turned, and the relief on his face said everything. He was going to get to hit somebody after all. The frustration burst out of him, and the betrayal, too. Leonard could see that especially, the betrayal.

It's a restaurant thing, he wanted to say, a kind of cook's code that you wouldn't understand. But he had no time to speak as Buck charged. Leonard pulled back to swing, and walking forward, he stepped right into the blow. It wasn't a roundhouse, which Leonard might have dodged. It was this fast jab from nowhere. Right off the man's chest. Pop. Leonard felt his nose crunch. Lightning shot in his eyes, and there was the sound of splintering rocks in his brain. He went down to one knee. There was blood in his nose. Blood poured down his face. It dripped through his fingers. And there was blood in his eyes, which he knew he had to wipe away before Buck could hit him again. But when he got to his feet and cleared them, he saw that Carla had come though the kitchen doors. She stood in the dining room, this chunky woman, short and kind of hefty at the same time. She had big muscles in her arms, and she was holding a meat cleaver in one hand. Her apron was covered in a spatter of grease and chicken guts. "You better just go find your dog, mister," she said.

θ

The dog man had come out of the diner to stand by his car again. He was cursing and shielding his eyes from the sun. Tessa and Hector were crouched behind the rough pink corner of the adobe church. They had watched the dog drink at the pot and then trot away, into the sage and down towards the cottonwoods and the river. The first time the man had come to gaze around the parking lot and the fields, he had called out, saying, "I know who you are, boy. You better get back here." A few people at the gas station had seemed mildly interested, but they had escaped unseen, and after a while the man returned to the diner. Tessa watched the traffic on the road. She saw her father coming from the steakhouse. He walked up to the BMW, where he squatted by the water and picked at the broken glass. He'd gone into the diner after that, and then the dog man came out again. He began to walk the perimeter of the parking lot.

This time he was calling for the dog. At the fence, he stopped and leaned on the gate post. He watched the goats in the shade of the shelter.

Hector took her hand and led her into the cool sanctuary of the church. Columns of dusty light cut the gloom. She gazed at the wooden figures in the *retablo*, Christ and the Virgin Mother, a dozen saints. They had been painted in the colors of the desert, purple shale and green sage. She walked the length of the pews to the altar, where she brushed her fingers along the chipped paint. It was very still inside, but through the doors, she could hear the man cursing, calling after his dog. There was silence for a while, and then he called again. He was louder this time, closer. He was coming up the road.

She grabbed Hector by the arm, and pulled him to a crouch. Outside, the man kept yelling. The flagstones felt cool on Tessa's knees, her palms. She crawled behind Hector to the aisle, where they could watch the doors. The dog man was standing there, facing outward. He was lit up in the full blaze of the day. Then slowly he turned, looking into the church. At first, he must not have seen them, or perhaps he didn't believe what it was he was seeing: two heads stacked one on top of the other. They were peering from beneath the pews. But presently, it registered, and he pointed at Hector. "You," he said. "I know you did it."

Some part of Tessa crumbled and gave way, as though her skin had suddenly slid down around her and left her bones exposed to the air. She was going to have to own up. But Hector stood. He pulled her to her feet. The stillness of the cool air crashed around them in the sanctuary, and she could hear Hector breathing out the seconds. Her heartbeat thundered in her chest. It echoed through the silence, as if the whole world throbbed with it. "Don't worry about him," said Hector. "He's just some stupid gringo."

The man stepped through the doorway and into the church. "What did you just say?"

Hector took her hand and pulled her to the wall. The man started down the aisle. They had to dodge him a few times, heading back to the altar as he came along the pews, but then breaking for it, they ran for the doors. He'd gotten tangled in the kneelers and he was blind angry, trying to climb over them and stumbling. He tripped and fell flat on the stone. Hector and Tessa ran into the bright sun. Her heart was pounding, and she pulled him to the road. But Hector threw her off. He turned and he raised both of his fists into the air. He locked his elbows. He shifted his weight and he planted his feet wide apart. Tessa's heart leapt into her throat. She grabbed at him, pulling for him to run, but he pushed her away. In the doors, the man struggled to his feet. Hector unfurled his two middle fingers, gave him his best double-eagles and yelled, "I said, fuck you, you stupid gringo piece of shit."

For an instant Hector held the pose, his chin jutting out and his face like a slab of hard granite. Then he grabbed Tessa by the hand and they set off at a dead run. She looked back once to see the man stagger from the church, where he tripped again in the gravel and split his knee. He looked purple from the neck up, as though his blood might burst a hole through the top of his head. Then they were gone. They ran through the yards, past the cars and the porches. They leapt a rusted clothes dryer, and they ducked under a line of wash. They dodged trees and weaved between trucks. They vaulted a fence and ran through a field, past the goats and sheep. Hector pointed to the cottonwoods at the river, and he led her back down the hill through the dirt yards of the rusty trailers. At a little eight-wide camper, they passed an old man in a nylon deck chair. He sat on a porch he had built himself out of plywood and breeze blocks. He waved to Hector as they ran.

By the time they got to the river, they could see no further sign of the man, and they stopped to breathe, bracing themselves against their knees. They looked at each other. Then Hector began to laugh, and after a moment, Tessa did, too. They wandered after that, along the water, searching in vain for the dog. But after a while they gave it up, and then

Hector took her to the base of the scarp, to a faint series of switchbacks that led to the top of the mesa. Up there, Tessa could look out over the town of Cerrito Blanco and down along the winding Rio Chama in the valley beyond. She could see the striated lines of the crumbling desert. The reservoir gleamed like a lost city in the distance. All around her the hot sun blazed in the sky above.

θ

Carla had given him a bag of ice, which Leonard held against his face as he walked across the highway to the Rio Chama Steakhouse. Jim stood in the parking lot, his eyes caged behind dark aviator shades. "Carla do that to you?" said Jim.

Leonard shook his head. "Some tourist."

"You want to call the police?"

"No," he said. Leonard had had a belly full of the police.

"So, what do you think?' said Jim. "Easy as pie."

"I'm having doubts," said Leonard.

"What doubts?"

"She gave me this ice," he said. Leaning his head back, he could taste the blood draining into his throat. "She's a pretty nice lady."

"This isn't personal," said Jim. "It's just business."

"So, why don't you go pull it?"

Jim put his arm around Leonard's shoulder. He touched his nose where it had begun to swell. "Really popped you one, didn't he?" he said. "Sure you don't want to call the cops?"

Leonard shook his head. "Only people I dislike more than cops are social workers," he said. There had been plenty of social workers after Darcy shot him. They interviewed both him and Tessa, separately and together, for hours on end and several times over. It was Darcy's mother who had put the social workers on him, claiming he was unfit.

That damned woman. She probably blamed him for the cheapness of the pistol, too. Jamming up like that, it had robbed her of the satisfaction that at least he was dead in the bargain.

"It's a matter of risk," said Jim. "What's at stake? See, if you screw up and get caught, you can just hop in that truck of yours and head on down the road. But what about me? I've got this business. I can't go anywhere. But listen, this isn't about me. I'll be okay even if I do have to let a few people go. This is about you and Tessa. Your futures. Because— look, I haven't told anybody about this, but I've got plans. Before she opened up the diner, I'd been thinking about expansion. Do you see what I'm saying? A business dies if it doesn't expand. So, I'm thinking about Santa Fe and I'm thinking about El Paso. You see? Hell, if we revamp the apps like you said, I'm thinking we can go all the way to Flagstaff and Phoenix. Shit man, what about Santa Monica? And, of course, I'm going to need a right-hand man. Somebody I can trust. You get me? Hell, we'll even take Carla back if you want to. You're right about her. She's a real nice lady. And she deserves better than some diner by the side of the road. So, you do this little thing for me, and I promise we'll take her back. Then we'll expand. Christ, she'll be making six-figures in a couple of years. You know we can do it. We cook the best goddamned steaks in New Mexico."

Leonard stood silent. He felt the breeze on his face, Jim's hand on his shoulder. "Yeah," he said. He nodded. "They're some damned good steaks, all right."

Jim clapped him on the back. When he'd left, Leonard remained in the parking lot, looking at the road and the desert, but eventually, there was nothing else for it, and he headed around to his trailer to change his smock. On the porch, he stopped to look for Tessa, but he didn't see her anywhere, so he figured she must have headed down to the river. He smelled the sage, and he listened to the wind scouring the rocks. There were birds in the sky, and he knew this was a better place for her than Denver. Him, too. It almost made him laugh, the thought of moving back with Darcy's mother. She'd been so pissed when Darcy pleaded guilty, because she would've loved to see Leonard on the stand. For Darcy, the plea meant the difference between five years and ten, but her mother maintained she would've done six months had the jury gotten a taste of Leonard. He wasn't entirely sure she was wrong.

In the trailer, he dug through the refrigerator for a Styrofoam box of old mac and cheese. Flies buzzed on the counter. He set the wire cutters aside, and he poured a stale cup of coffee. He was sweating in the heat, which Darcy had always detested. Idly, he wondered if she had the AC up there at the women's facility in Denver. This quick burst of pleasure opened up in his heart when he thought about her sitting alone in that concrete box, miserable in the heat and terrified. But then his heart exploded, and he felt only pain and self-pity, and he began to cry. Tears poured down his face, and he cried and cried. He let his sorrow roll through him and all the suffering, which somebody had once told him was the clay of life itself, the very substrate of time and space. "It's okay," he said, aloud. He held his arms around his shoulders. He sat on the floor and he pulled his knees to his chest. "It's all right to feel like this," he said. "It's just a little game you're playing with yourself, because you don't really love her still." Then he rolled to his side and lay on the linoleum, and he watched the blood on the floor, pooling around his eye. He longed only to hold her again. If he could just hold her once more, like he had on their wedding night. She'd wore this black slip, and it felt like water flowing over his fingers. He wished he could feel her nails digging into his back again. And how she was drenched in sweat and laughing that night when they had stood on the retaining wall in New Orleans with that silk scarf around her neck. The winds were just picking up, and those clouds came rolling in. She'd jumped into his arms, and they'd rolled through the French Quarter. They ate etouffée and drank shots of Dickel, and they danced all night and it was four in the morning and they hadn't been able to stop dancing to that Delta blues.

Leonard wiped his face, his tears. He wiped the blood and the mucus off the back of his hands. It was like his heart had gotten clapped in the door somewhere, and it was still there, stuck and beating and distant, a heart gone to him now and lost forever. He rolled to his back. He stared at the ceiling, listening to the flies in the sink. After a while, he sat up and pulled out of his shirt. He dug around in a pile of clothes for another chef's smock. In the bathroom, he cleaned himself up. He stuffed the wire cutters into his back pocket and grabbed the mac and cheese off the counter.

Outside, he was heading into the yard, when he stopped short at the sight of the dog. It was a short-haired dog, with a boxy face, and flecks of orange and black running through the coat. He knelt in the dust. "I bet you're that asshole's dog," he said. "You want some of this mac and cheese?" He set the container on the ground and squatted back on his haunches. The dog sniffed it, eyed him for a moment and then ate, whining with the pleasure of the food. Leonard scratched it behind the ears, and when it was finished eating—she—she rolled to her back so he could rub her belly. He looked to the gas station and Carla's Diner, the cars in the parking lot. "You can stay in my trailer," he said. "I'll bring you some more to eat when I get off work." But as he stood, the dog rolled to her feet. She bolted into the field and ran down towards the river.

θ

At the top of the mesa, Tessa listened to the scrub brush rattling in the breeze. She could feel the sun on her face. She watched a police cruiser pull into the parking lot at Carla's Diner. The officer looked so small in the distance, talking with the man. Carla had come out with them, and the three stood in conference together. There were a lot of shrugs from Carla and the officer, and with each shrug the man seemed to get more irate, until finally he packed himself back into the BMW and left. She watched him on the highway until he was gone. She did not think that he had found his dog.

Hector took her along the mesa to a place where the top layer of sediment had crumbled down the side of the scarp. A screwdriver lay in the dirt, along with a ballpeen hammer. He squatted in the dust, Pointing, he showed her where the end of a great petrified bone stuck out from the rock. She knelt and traced it with her finger. Thick as her leg, the bone looked much darker than the surrounding mudstone. Hector picked up the screwdriver. He jabbed it into the dirt, splintering flecks off the rock. Then he took the hammer, and he began to tap at the screwdriver. "I'm going to uncover this whole thing," he said.

"What do you think it is?" Tessa sat cross-legged beside him.

"I think it's a dragon," said Hector. She looked at the hard ground, trying to imagine the bones of some massive beast stretching beneath the stone. "Actually, I bet it's some kind of sauropod," he said. "It'll take me years to dig it up, but then I'm going to sell it and buy my mother a new house. Then she won't have to work so much in the diner."

"What's it worth?" said Tessa.

He shrugged. "Could be worth millions," he said.

"Can I help?" He handed her the screwdriver and the hammer. Tessa set the blade against the rock and tapped it.

All afternoon they took turns chiseling at the rock. It was a hot day while they worked. She felt slick with sweat. And Hector told her about the dinosaurs and the great sweep of time that could still be read in the rocks of that land. "There used to be a forest of palm trees here," he said. "A long time ago. Swamps full of cypress trees and massive vines." It was all a painted desert of crumbling rock now. But Hector said that after the swamps there had come an age of great sand dunes. They had stretched from Colorado all the way to Mexico. Then, over the eons, they had settled into the crumbling sandstone, which he pointed out to her in the striated lines of the ridges. But in turn, that world was overcome, swept clean by the waters of a vast inland sea. Above the valley, a baroque dream of huge worms twisted in the sky. She saw the great beasts lumbering along the shore. Bats, the size of horses, cruised overhead. Sediment had layered into sediment, and the stone had covered it over. She could see all around her the whole myth of the Earth itself, the whole history of the world, written in siltstone and shale. There was dust in her nose and between her teeth. Her scalp itched with the grit. She picked up a piece of mudstone, and with the tip of her finger, she traced the network of burrows, where a hundred million years ago tiny creatures had lived out the sum total of their tiny lives.

By the evening, when the shadows had grown long in the desert light, they'd cleared away about a foot of rock. Around them every pebble cast a finger of darkness along the ground. Tessa sat cross-legged near the edge of the scarp. The tools lay in the dirt beside her. She had stopped to admire the sun and the red desert that stretched beyond the green banks of the Rio Chama. The hot wind blew in her hair, and she could feel the grit of the dust all over her body.

"Why are you crying?" said Hector. It was only then that she realized she had been crying and that her face was wet with dirty tears. Tears had streaked her cheeks. She wrapped her arms around her legs and laid her face in her knees. He sat beside her with his arm around her shoulder. They watched the sun on the far horizon. There was orange light on the river and in the sky. "What's the matter?" he said.

"Nothing," she said. "I was just thinking about something, but it's not important. I should probably get home. Can we come up here again tomorrow? And dig more?"

"Whenever you want," he said. He patted her knee with his

small dirty fingers. "I don't have a lot of friends who are interested in paleontology. Most everyone I know are assholes."

"That's true all over," she said. "Most everybody you meet, they're going to be an asshole."

θ

It was well past dusk when they returned to the diner, where Hector waved goodbye. She knew she ought to get home, but she lingered in the parking lot for a while. She stood in the glow of the security lights. Through the windows, she watched Carla mopping the floor along the booths. Hector sat on one of the stools, and Carla put her mop aside. She kissed his forehead, and she walked behind the counter, where she brought up a small plate with a crumpled piece of pie. This she set in front of Hector, along with a fork and a napkin. They talked for a bit, Carla looking skeptical. But he kept grinning the whole time, gesturing with his hands, pointing and telling, she supposed, the whole saga of the chase through the yards of Cerrito Blanco. But, no. He shook his head. No way. That stupid gringo didn't know what he was talking about.

After a while, Carla gave up the interrogation. She ruffled his hair and went over to the jukebox, where she slid a dollar into the machine. She punched a few buttons and then returned to her mop. In the parking lot, Tessa stood rooted to the ground. She had begun to cry again, and she found now that she could not stop. Carla took up her mop, and she began to sway as she made her way slowly through the dining room. Still sobbing, Tessa had turned to go when she saw the shadows moving beside the diner. It was only a rustle in the gravel, and at first she thought it was the dog or the man again, come back to kill her. Her heart jumped, and she turned to run, but it wasn't the dog or the man either. It was her father. It was Leonard. He was doing something where the power lines came down from the pole. She squatted in the gravel.

Inside the diner, Hector had slipped off the stool. Carla set the mop aside, and he stood on her feet, while she danced him around the room. He was too big for it, but she lugged him through the air as best she could. They stumbled through the doors and into the kitchen. Tessa heard the scrape of metal where her father had pulled the meter housing loose. She looked at the empty counter, the swinging doors, and the kitchen beyond. It was anger that hit her, full in the chest. She stomped through the gravel, and he must've heard her coming, because he dropped something in the dirt. He bent to scramble for it and snatched up a set of wire cutters.

"What are you doing?" she said.

"I told you not to come over here."

"Are you trying to shut their power off?"

Leonard looked at the meter, as if perhaps he did not know what it was, nor what he intended. "Listen," he said. "You are the child. I am the parent. I told you not to cross that highway and you did. Now, you're grounded."

"Grounded?" she said. She pointed at the meter. "You're going to ground me?"

"This is not the important thing here," he said. "The important thing is that you need to get back across that road and into that trailer. I don't have time to explain right now, but when I get back, we'll talk about your punishment."

"What's the matter with you?" she said. "You can't go shutting off people's power."

"You're just a child," he said. "You're not going to understand, but I don't have a choice if we want to keep this job. So, maybe you don't have to be grounded this time. Maybe this can just be a warning."

"You're calling me the child?" she said. "Is this some kind of prank?"

"I'm not the child," he said. "You are. Now, go home."

He took hold of the meter and began to rock it off the pins.

"If you do it," she said. "I'm leaving."

He stopped. He put his hands on his hips. "What do you mean, you're leaving?"

"I'll go back to Denver," she said.

"I guess you're planning to hitchhike."

"Men would pick me up," she said. "Don't you think?"

He almost slapped her then. She could see it in his eyes.

"I'll just start walking," she said. "I'll walk right down that road there, and I'll get into the first car that stops. I'll say, take me to Denver, mister. There's kids who do it all the time. And you know what else? Their parents don't care. You wouldn't. You'd be like, good riddance."

"Of course, I care," he said. "What's the matter with you, anyway?"

"What's the matter with me?" she said. "What's the matter with you?"

"And don't think I don't know about that dog," he said. "You put a chunk of concrete through that man's window. Look at this. He punched me in the face." Leonard leaned down so she could see his mashed nose.

"Ouch," she said, and she felt instantly sorry for him. She touched his cheek. Dark bruises had begun to swell around both of his eyes. "Let's just go back to the trailer."

"Jim's going to let me go if I don't do this," he said. "Do you understand what that means?"

"Then screw Jim," she said. "I—look—Dad—I met this boy, Carla's son. His name is Hector, and he's probably eleven and we like saved that dog's life. Then we hiked around and we went up on the mesa there where we're digging up a dinosaur bone. And it's just like you said it would be. It's this massive bone. It's right in the ground and I spent the whole day up there and—"

"I'm sorry," he said. "But I have to do it. This boy—Hector—he'll still be around. He's not going anywhere. Jim says he'll hire Carla back at the steakhouse, anyway. And he says once business gets going again, he'll need a right-hand man out in Santa Monica."

"But I could never be friends with Hector after this."

"It's not like he'll know," he said.

"I'll know," she said. "I'm not like that. I'm not like you. I'm not ever going to be like you. Not ever in a million years."

She turned away and stomped through the gravel to the highway, where she began to walk westward, in her tank top and shorts. There were a few cars on the road, but Leonard did not think that she would stop one. He watched her go. She was about fifty yards away and still under the lights from the gas station. There, she stopped. She looked back at him once, waiting in the shadows beside the diner. She stood by the road, and as a car passed, she jammed her thumb out. But she was too late that time. The car sped on up the highway. She was just showing that she was capable of it. She'd do it eventually. That's what she wanted him to see. She'd get into some car one of these days. It was a kind of hurling of herself into the abyss if he didn't do as she demanded, the goddamned child. With a scowl, he walked after her and then jogged, as more lights appeared in the gloom.

At the road, he grabbed her shoulder and jerked her around. Bats flew in the darkness overhead. She had been crying, and she looked bloodless and grey. Her face was streaked with dirty sweat and tears. But she wouldn't let him touch her. She shook free and stood defiant. He thought he was going to have to pick her up, drag her back to the trailer. But he'd have to lock her in her room and keep her tied up all the time. It wasn't possible. And it suddenly hit him that she was free. She was her own person now and no longer his little girl at all. She was only thirteen years old. She wasn't an adult. No, she couldn't possibly be free, and yet there she was. She had freed herself. She would leave him soon. Then probably he would never see her again. There were tears in her eyes. Her face looked a mess, and he reached out to touch her hair where he'd hacked it off with his clippers. She was just a little girl, but she had already left him.

Most children did that at sixteen or seventeen. That's when they separate. But Tessa had done it at thirteen. And then suddenly he saw himself, in some lonely future, wandering the corridors of a state hospital. It was not so many years down the line. He was shuffling along, heading out to the waiting room. She'd be there with her husband and some children of her own. She wouldn't hug him. He could see the hard twist of her mouth as she mumbled hello. Goddamned Darcy would be out of jail, the two of them reconciled, bonded. Hell, Darcy would probably have come out to the state hospital with her.

"Tell me about this dinosaur bone," he said.

He wiped at his tears, and the headlights grew large on the highway.

"Are you going to shut off the power?"

"No."

Tessa fell around him. She pressed her face into his stomach. Gripping him around the arms, she held him as tight as she could. She was shaking, trembling. Her long, gawky arms quaked as she held him. He pulled his hands loose and he mashed her head against his chest. She had begun to sob, and she was his little girl again. At least for a while. He watched the approaching car over the top of her head. He was thinking about the people in it. What monsters they were. To drive along country roads and pick up lost girls. He felt a surge of hatred. Then the car slowed. It rolled to a stop at the shoulder. He balled up his fists and glared at the driver. It was Buck in that BMW. When Tessa saw him, she ducked behind Leonard's back.

"You're that fellow I whacked today," said Buck.

"That's right," said Leonard. "You want to get out of that car and try it again?"

"No," he said. "I just want my goddamned dog. You haven't seen a dog, have you?"

"No," said Leonard. "I haven't seen any dog."

"What about you?" he said. "Are you that girl I saw today?"

"You don't talk to her," said Leonard. "You ever talk to her again and I'll kill you."

Buck drove off, leaving them by the side of the road. Leonard put his arm around her and ran his fingers through the stubble on her head. "I'm sorry I fucked up your hair," he said.

"It's no big deal," she said.

"It is a big deal," he said. "We'll have more money someday. I've just got to figure out how. Why don't you tell me about this dinosaur bone?"

Tessa pulled away from him. She took his hand, he dropped the wire cutters in the ditch, and she led him up the dirt road to the switchbacks. In the darkness, they hiked to the top of the mesa. There was a good moon, and she brought him down to the edge where the bone stuck from the earth. They squatted together and poked it with their fingers.

"You and that boy dug it up?"

"I was going to come back tomorrow," she said. "But I guess I won't now. Will I?"

They sat together on the ground. "We'll be moving on," he said. "We could go to Texas."

The screwdriver still lay in the dirt where they had left it next to the hammer. Tessa picked it up. She scraped along the edge of the bone. She picked up the hammer, which she liked the feel of in her hand, and she looked at the highway twisting through the eroded cliffs. Red taillights winked out around the bend. She would not have gotten into the car if it had stopped. But what if a car did stop? What if it was the man with the dog, foul and dank? But then, it might have been some boy, too. It might be a smart boy like Hector, though probably it would be one of those loser boys, like the ones at her grandmother's apartment complex in Denver. The ones who like to huff Rush and see how long they can go without breathing. Or maybe it wouldn't be a boy at all. Maybe it was some girl that she was going to meet in school that year. Some older girl with a car all her own and tattoos of Hello Kitty on her shoulders. Some dream of the hippie life out there in places like Portland and Seattle. But then again, maybe it wouldn't be anyone at all. Maybe there was just her. Only Tessa. With a car door all her own. It could happen one night as she walked out of the 7-Eleven, that she would find an open car door, keys still in the ignition, the engine running, and beneath her a road that rolled on out to nowhere. She dropped the screwdriver and hammer. "Or we could go back to Denver," she said.

Leonard looked at her in the darkness, the light of the moon on her face. She looked just like Darcy used to look. From behind them, they heard a scrambling in the rocks. The dog had followed them up the mesa, and it came and sat beside them. It sniffed at the bone, their feet. Tessa ran her fingers along the dog's back. She put her arm around its neck and lay against its head. Leonard stood. He walked away from the edge of the mesa. He kicked at the stones, and he looked into the sky. There were stars all around them, the Milky Way bright and clear. It stretched from horizon to horizon. And he was going to end up in that lonely state hospital, anyway. Because everyone does. Your wife shoots you in the stomach, your children abandon you, and your friends all turn out to be thieves. Still, there are stars in the night sky in New Mexico. Darcy's mother couldn't take that away.

"You want me to go stay with Darcy's mother?" he said. "She hates me."

"She doesn't hate you," said Tessa. "She told me herself that she loves you like a son."

And he could see the lights of that 7-Eleven where he was doomed to work the graveyard shift if they went back to Denver. He could see that hateful old woman screaming at him to get off the couch and drive Tessa down to the Women's Facility to go see Darcy. They'd walk through the metal detectors to the family room together. "I know she does," he said.

"Maybe life's not all about you," she said.

"Well, it's not all about you either," he said.

Tessa touched the bone. She crossed her legs, and the dog lay down beside her. They could hear the river and the cars on the highway. The light went on in the trailer behind Carla's, and Leonard squatted beside her in the dirt. He touched her fingers while she traced the bone. "This guy died a hundred million years ago," said Tessa. "Hector says it was all a jungle here then. But look at it now. You know what's weird, though? It's all still here, all the plants and the trees and the ferns and the cypresses and all those climbing vines and all that swampy ground. Those triceratops. Those T-Rexes. All those allosauruses and pterodactyls. All the monsters of the Earth's long childhood. They're all still here. Fossilized and frozen if you know where to look."

"Your mother's going to be in jail for another five years," he said.

"Grandmother says she'll get out in three."

"She's not allowed to see you."

"But you could change that if you wanted."

"I don't want to change it."

"I wouldn't ever leave you for her," she said.

"You almost left me tonight," he said. "You were going to get into some passing car."

"But you wouldn't have let me," she said. "I knew you wouldn't."

"So, you've forgiven your mother, then?" he said. "Is that it?"

"Haven't you?" she said.

And they sat for a long while, watching the stars overhead and the moon as it slowly tracked across the sky. After a while, Leonard twisted the collar on the dog to look at the name, the phone number. Then he unbuckled it. He pulled the strap through the metal loop, and he tossed it off the mesa, where it clattered in the stones below.

About the Author

Born in Maryland, Charley Henley bounced around as a child, living everywhere from a back-to-the-land community in Eastern Washington to rural Rankin County, Mississippi, disparate locales and people that have fueled the stories of this present volume. He attended the University of Montana, studying philosophy, working in restaurants, and wandering in the woods. His work has appeared in *Best New American Voices*, *The Greensboro Review*, and *Copper Nickel*, among other places. Currently, he lives with his wife and children in the Seattle area. He teaches at the University of Cincinnati. *The Deep Code* is his debut collection of short stories.